The King Cartel 2

Frank Gresham

Lock Down Publications
Presents
The King Cartel 2
Truth and Consequences
A Novel by *Frank Gresham*

Frank Gresham

Lock Down Publications
P.O. Box 1482
Pine Lake, Ga 30072-1482

Lock Down Publications
Facebook: Author Frank Gresham
Like our page on Facebook: Lock Down Publications @
www.facebook.com/lockdownpublications.ldp
Cover design and layout by: **Dynasty's Cover Me**
Book interior design by: **Shawn Walker**
Edited by: **Mia Rucker**

Acknowledgement

First, I would like to give a humble thanks to God.

To my loving and supporting family and to my loyal partner, Renee Lamb. Her patience, commitment, love and belief in me has played a major part in my growth and success. Thank you very much.

And a special thanks and shout out to Ca$h and my LDP family. (We taking over). And to all the book clubs and loyal fans, thanks a million. Your support and friendship is greatly appreciated.

"Some people aren't loyal to you. They are loyal to their need of you. Once their needs change, so does their loyalty."

Dedication

Tony Gresham, Keith Gresham, Antonio 'Booty' Gresham, Johnny 'Stank' Williams, Kendrick Rakestraw and Julius 'Hook' Rakestraw. R.I.P. Always on my mind, forever in my heart!!!

Frank Gresham

Introduction

Wednesday

Damar was sleeping fitfully tossing and turning in his first class seat on the flight home to his mother's funeral. He was dreaming about the last time he saw her at the nursing home. She looked so happy and peaceful but now she was gone. The stewardess came over the intercom thanking everyone for flying Delta Airline.

Damar sat up and unfastened his seatbelt. He grabbed his phone and saw he had a missed call from Gava, his drug supplier, so he hit him back to see what was up.

Gava picked up on the second ring.

"Gwan mi breda," Gava said in his dialect meaning, *What's going on, my brother?*

"Shit, 'bout to step off the plane. What's up wit'cha?"

"I hear you de boss in Miami. You tryin' to take *mi* spot a hoe?"

"Nah, I ain't trying to take nobody spot. I'm just handling my business and taking care of mines. Where you going with this, my nigga?"

"Rude boy, I have a proposition fa ya. I want thirty percent of your take in Miami. Good 'ting is I'ma front you two thousand keys, and give me ten stacks off of each."

Damar assumed this was a joke and almost forgot to laugh.

"Ha ha, nigga, get the fuck outta here. That ain't no proposition. That's greed, mutha'fucka. On the real though, what's up? What you call me for? 'Cause right now ain't the time to be fuckin' wit' a nigga, you feel me?"

Damar thought Gava was just bullshitting, but he wasn't. He was dead serious. By Damar's insulting reply, Gava figured he thought he was joking so he let it be known that he meant business.

"Rude boy, you have no choice in de matta. Either thirty percent or Gava take everyting, even your life."

"What the fuck?" Damar asked and stood up.

He couldn't believe Gava tried him like a sucka.

"Mutha'fucka, did a coconut fall on your damn head? Do you know who the fuck I am?" Damar hissed through the phone.

Gava growled back into the phone. "Grrr pussy clot mon."

Damar put his mouth closer to the receiver. "Nigga, what the fuck did you just call me?"

"*Pussyclot, pussyclot.* You cunt hear? If Gava have to come to de states, you and your family will disappear."

Damar frowned and bit down on his bottom lip.

"Nigga, suck my dick 'cause I ain't giving you shit. And if you touch anything of mines, you fake ass Jamaican, I will cut yo' bitch ass up into little pieces and feed you to the iguanas."

He ended the call.

Damar was furious when he turned to step into the alleyway. A passenger accidently bumped into him. Off of impulse, he pushed the man down to the floor. "Watch where the fuck you going."

Chapter 1

The parking lot at Popular Springs Baptist Church was jammed packed just as Damar thought it would be. He slowly pulled his rental car to the rear of the church. He dreaded this gloomy day, the day he would see his mother, Patricia King, for the last time. He was almost an hour late due to traffic.

He whipped the Benz in behind a white sedan and parallel parked under an oak tree. He reached inside his coat pocket and pulled out a flask of vodka, spun the top off, and took two sips before placing it under the seat. Then he tossed a couple of mints in his mouth and stepped out of the car dressed in all-black with a pair of cardigan shades on.

He made his way to the front entrance of the church. At the top of the steps, he took a long deep breath and then proceeded through the double doors. Due to the fact that he was the last to arrive, more than a few heads turned to look at him. Damar kept a straight face as he peered back at them.

One of the ushers greeted him with a smile and handed him an obituary. Damar thanked her then paused for a second and looked at his beloved mother's photo. It was one she'd taken a couple of years back before she got sick. Her smile was as bright as the sun and happiness was written all over her face.

Damar sighed then walked up the aisle and attempted to sit on the front row, but a deacon touched his elbow then leaned over and whispered, "This row is for family only."

Damar took a seat on the third row. Deacon Wayne Lay had just read a bible scripture from the Old Testament followed by the choir's musical selection.

Damar's mother had four sisters and one brother and that was Uncle Henry. The sisters all sat on the front row holding hands and weeping over their big sister. Damar then peered around looking for Uncle Henry, Aunt Teresa, and Mario Junior who he thought would have been on the front row, but they weren't. So he looked over to the other side of the church and spotted his uncle on the second row wearing a grey suit. Aunt Teresa was snuggled up next to him in a turquoise dress with the hat to match. Mario Junior had on a white button up and was rocking a Mohawk. Damar couldn't fathom what was on Junior's mind since he was the only grandchild. At that moment, a glint of sunlight beamed between the pews. Damar turned around and saw his nemesis walk through the door and take a seat. He couldn't believe his eyes. *Damn, they musta tapped my phone*, Damar thought to himself.

Damar was so heated he started to go back there and beat his bitch ass to death with his bare hands. If it had it been somebody else's funeral besides his mother's, he would have. Instead of acting irrationally, he laced his fingers together, but it didn't stop his trigger finger from itching.

"This is the last straw, mutha'fucka. One of us gon' die today," Damar said under his breath as he turned his attention back to the choir.

When the choir finished, Pastor Eugene Cooper stepped up to the pulpit in a black robe. The deacon kindly took a seat next to the choir. After adjusting the microphone, the pastor greeted the church and went into the eulogy. There wasn't a dry eye in the church. Patricia was loved by everyone. He then recited a poem requested by the family.

"God saw you were getting tired and a cure wasn't meant to be so he put his arms around you and whispered, *Come to me*."

Damar's anger subsided as the pastor read the heartfelt poem. It didn't change his mind about doing what had to be done once and for all. *You have to be one cocky mutha'fucka to come to my mama's funeral,* Damar thought to himself.

After the poem, Sister Lila Jackson read the acknowledgement as the pallbearers came and stood to the left of the casket. Starting at the back row, everyone came up and paid their last respects to

Patricia. Damar's mom had lived a hard working but a good life and she had touched so many people with her love and kindness, despite her own hardships. Damar waited patiently while friends, family and people of different races walked passed him and viewed the body.

When the last person walked by, the elderly sisters of the church started humming an old tune. Damar couldn't remember the name of it but he remembered hearing the song as a child. As everyone exited the church and headed to the gravesite, Damar walked over to the casket just as one of the pallbearer's was closing it.

"Wait," he said as he touched the man's shoulder.

"Give me two minutes?" he asked.

The man nodded, opened the casket, and stepped next to the pallbearers.

Damar removed his shades and placed a hand on top of his mother's hand.

"Hey, mama, it's me. You look real good," Damar said as he rubbed her hand. "Damn, I never thought you would go before me, never. Mama, I'm sorry for all the bullshit I put you through. I'm also sorry for not spending time with you during your illness. I know you loved me very much. I know this and I just hope and pray you forgive me for being who I am. One more thing, mama, before I let you rest. As long as I live, there willl never be a woman alive that could ever take your place."

Damar then reached in his coat and took out a white rose and laid it on his mother before closing the casket. The pallbearers gathered around the burgundy casket and proceeded towards the door. Damar slid his shades on and followed them outside. While they were going down the steps, he saw his arch enemy standing by his car door looking around.

"You don't see me, but I see you mutha'fucka," Damar said, under his breath.

A moment after realizing that Damar wasn't at the service, or so he thought, the man cut his losses then got into his car and pulled off.

Damar looked at the church, and then at the taillights leaving the parking lot.

He then glanced up at the grey sky. "Sorry, mama, but this gotta end today. I love you."

Then he trotted to his car and followed the vehicle into Athens and to the *Hampton Inn*. He whipped his rental into the *McDonald's* parking lot next to the hotel. He watched the man get out of his car, grab a small luggage bag out of the trunk, and then go into the hotel lobby. While Damar sat in his car plotting, he didn't know his sister Valerie was two miles away at *Athens Regional Medical Center*. She was admitted two weeks prior to their mother's death. The HIV virus she contracted from having unprotected sex had progressed into full blown AIDS and the doctors gave her less than six months to live. Even though she was dying, she still refused to contact any of her family members. When asked by the medical staff, she told them she had no family to ensure they didn't call against her wishes.

***

Meanwhile Back In Miami

Oga, Taz, and Lucky were serving all the high end dealers with the Cartel's coke just as Damar instructed them to do before he left to go to his mother's funeral.

His cousin, Fresh, caught a late flight to Georgia but not to Damar's knowledge. He flew in to check on his girl, Cassie. Dub Sac and Boo Boo were at Damar's water front mansion on West 27th Street watching Jamerica until he returned.

Jamerica was lying across her king size bed watching a movie, while talking to her girlfriend Tamika.

"*Whoo,* girl, let me name the baby," Tamika said, excitedly just after hearing the good news that Jamerica was expecting.

"Bitch, please, you ain't giving my baby no ghetto name and I don't know what I'm having anyway. My doctor's appointment ain't until Friday."

"I say it's gonna be a boy so how 'bout Prince?" Tamika asked.

"Ummm, Prince. Prince Damar King. I kinda like that." Jamerica said as she rolled over on her back.

"Oh, oh, oh, or you can name him Teriyaki," Tamika blurted out.

"*Girl*, my child will not be named after no damn food. I'll stick with Prince for now. That is if it's a boy, but if it's a girl I'm going to name her Alexandria."

"Oh no, I don't like dat. Hell to the naw," Tamika said, frowning up at the phone.

"Too bad, bitch, 'cause this ain't your baby," Jamerica then got out of bed. "Hold on, girl, I gotta use the bathroom."

Downstairs Boo Boo and Dub Sac were going at it on the big screen playing Madden 25. Dub Sac was sitting on the floor higher than usual, leaning to one side vigorously while pressing the controller. Boo Boo's quarterback was running for a twenty yard touchdown. Boo Boo stood up as his man dove into the end zone.

"Yeah, yeah, yeah, nigga," Boo Boo yelled.

Dub Sac tossed the controller and got up from the floor.

"Man, dis some fuck shit."

He left the room and went back to the pool.

Boo Boo chuckled right when his phone rang. It was his girl, Shonda.

"What up, boo?" He stood up and then plopped on the couch.

"Hey hell, mutha'fucka. Where the hell you at?" Shonda screamed through the phone.

Boo Boo held the phone away from his ear while she continued to yell. When she stopped to catch her breath, Boo Boo put the phone back to his ear.

"Can I talk now? Alright, let's try this shit again, Shonda. What's up, baby?"

"What the fuck you think up? You said you were flying in with your boss man. Now here it is going on eleven thirty and yo' fat ass ain't nowhere to be found."

"Yea, I know. But at the last minute, my boss man, as you would say, wanted me and Dub Sac to watch his girl while he was gone. That's why I'm not there."

"So you mean to tell me that you didn't bring your ass home because you had to watch another nigga's *bitch*. Bye, Boo Boo."

"Girl, you betta not hang up on me."

"What, Boo Boo? What?"

"Shut the fuck up and listen. As soon as he gets back, I will be on the first thing smoking. I promise. Now chill ya hyper ass out."

He heard her sigh through the phone.

"Don't lie to me, Boo Boo. Do you promise?"

"Yeah, yeah, I promise, baby." Boo Boo was ready to hang up the phone now.

"Fuck dat nigga," Shonda's friend, Tam, yelled over her shoulder as she walked past her heading to the kitchen.

Boo Boo recognized Tam's big mouth. He didn't like her because she was the biggest hoe in Athens and he told Shonda he didn't want her over to their house.

"You tell that bitch, Tam, to suck my dick and to get the fuck out my house. She betta not be there when I get home. You hear me, Shonda?"

"Well, you ain't here so somebody gotta keep me company," she replied.

"Them kids all the company yo' ass need. Now tell that hoe to see her way out the door," Boo Boo said.

"Okay, I will, just bring your ass home."

"A'ight, baby, I'ma talk to you later. I'm 'bout to grab me something to eat."

"Bye, boy," then she added, "ole greedy ass nigga."

Boo Boo heard the smart remark and shot back his own response although she'd already hung up. "*Shit!* Yo' ass greedy too," he said, walking into the kitchen.

Frank Gresham

Chapter 2

By nightfall, Damar had dosed off in his rental while staking out Detective Goldman at his hotel.

Pussy clot, if Gava have to come to de states, you and your family will disappear. Gava's threat echoed in Damar's ear, causing him to twitch in his sleep. Suddenly, someone or something bumped into his car and he woke up breathing heavily.

"What the fuck?" he asked and looked back to the rear of his car.

It was an old school cat with a perm, wearing black slacks and a brown shirt. He was pushing around a young lady that was carrying a toddler. She was up against the car with her head down taking the abuse while the child cried. Damar had seen all he needed to see before he jumped out of his car and went to her rescue.

"Hey, my nigga, hit on somebody who gon' hit back," Damar said, mean mugging with his left hand cocked back ready to knock the nigga's block off.

The guy turned and noticed Damar's left fist to the side of him and this made him angrier. He walked over to Damar and he could see that he had a mouth full of gold teeth.

"Nigga, I know you ain't checking me about my bi—"

That was all he got out his mouth before Damar threw a lightning fast right jab straight to his jaw. The guy dropped instantly. He went one way and his pullout grill went the other. *Ching a ling-ling* was the sound it made as it bounced under Damar's car. Damar had squirreled his ass with the old fake move like he was going to hit him with the left. So ole dude never saw the right that knocked him out cold. Damar smirked as he walked over to the girl. He knew he had flat lined a nigga with the oldest trick in the book.

"Hey, shawty, you a'ight?" Damar asked the girl who looked like she was somewhere in her twenties, but she was actually eighteen.

She was brown skinned, standing around 5'6", wearing clothes that appeared to be a little bit too tight.

"Yeah, I'm alright," she said barely over a whisper as she caressed her little boy's head.

The little boy had stopped crying and was now wiping his eyes dry.

Damar pointed to the man on the ground. "Is that yo' nigga?"

The girl lowered her head in shame. She knew the man lying on the ground looked old enough to be her damn granddaddy.

"Something like that," she finally said after Damar stood there for a minute.

By her late response and her facial expression, Damar knew it could only be one of two things. The nigga had to be her suga daddy or her pimp, and Damar didn't like either one.

"Hey, shawty, it's getting late. Where you staying at? I can drop you off," Damar asked, and gently touched her shoulder to show he meant no aggression.

"With him," she looked down at the unconscious man.

"Why was he pushing on you?"

"We just came out to eat and he said that I was looking at some dude—"

"Hold up, shawty," Damar cut in. "I don't care what you did. Him pushing you around and calling you out yo' name in front of your seed don't justify nothing. He's a coward, you feel me? If you stay with him, he's just gonna keep hitting on you."

The girl pulled her baby boy closer onto her bosom.

"But we ain't got nowhere to go."

"I know you got some family somewhere, don't you?"

"Yeah, I do, but they live in Jacksonville, Florida."

"Why don't you go there?"

"Because I ran away when I was sixteen."

"Why?"

"When I got pregnant, my mama was going to make me have an abortion and I wasn't gonna kill my baby for nobody."

"Come here."

Damar wrapped his arms around them for a brief moment. Then he held her by the shoulders.

"Look at me." She raised her little head and Damar saw the confusion and pain in her young eyes. "Listen, I'm heading back to Miami tomorrow. Let me take you home, a'ight? A young lady ain't got no business out here all alone."

Realizing her rescuer spoke the truth of her situation, she nodded *yes* and whispered, "Okay."

Damar glanced off to his side and noticed Detective Goldman coming out of the hotel Damar suddenly grabbed the girl by her arm, opened the passenger door to his car and ushered her inside. He told her to get in. She quickly got in and put her son next to her. Damar ran around the car and got in.

She could tell by Damar's sudden apprehension that it was best to go along with the flow without asking questions, so instinctually, she got in. Damar then hustled to the other side, giving life to the engine.

Detective Goldman pulled into traffic and went south on West Broad Street toward downtown. Damar did the same, driving behind him but with undetectable distance between them.

"Hey, shawty, y'all scrap up, a'ight?"

She nodded her obedience and quickly fastened the seatbelt for her son, who she placed in the backseat, and then herself.

Damar weaved through traffic to ensure he didn't lose the detective.

Damar then caught a glimpse of the young girl's face as he was switching to the right lane. She was nervous and for good reason.

She was with a stranger who was pushing eighty on the highway, going only God knows where.

To break the tension, he opened up dialogue. "Hey, I'm Carl, by the way. What's your name?"

"Kim," she answered as stiffly as her body looked.

"Ease up, shawty. You gon' be a'ight." She relaxed a little when she saw a smile break across his lips. He then pointed behind them. "And what's lil man's name and how old is he?"

"His name is Tyler and he's two."

"Cute son."

Now, she smiled. "Thank you."

Refocusing on the detective, he saw him get off on the nearing exit. With two cars in front of him, he did the same.

He then followed Goldman a quarter mile before he pulled into *Red Lobster's* parking lot. Driving up to the entrance, he quickly hopped out and went inside.

Damar inconspicuously parked at the other end.

Out of curiosity, Kim asked, "What you following him for?"

Damar looked Kim squarely in the eyes. "He ticked me off in the worst way." Then he turned the radio station to V103. *Lifestyle* by Rich Gang was playing and little Tyler started bobbing his little head. "Go, lil man." Damar smiled and began bobbing his head, too.

Damar was looking at Tyler dancing and didn't see the detective when he got back into his car and drove off, but Kim did. She tapped him on the shoulder.

"Yeah, what's up, shawty?" he asked.

Kim just pointed at Goldman's car going back up West Broad Street.

"Shit!" Damar said and put the car in drive.

He followed Detective Goldman and ended up right back at the hotel. This time he parked in the hotel's parking lot two cars over from the detective. Detective Goldman stepped out of his car with a carry out box and went back inside.

Damar rubbed his chin as he conjured up another plan.

"Um, let me see, let me see," he said out loud. "Hey, Kim, I'ma need you to follow dude and see what room he's in."

Without saying a word, Kim quickly removed her seatbelt and then her son's. She grabbed Tyler and hopped out of the car. As fast as she moved, Damar could tell she was used to being told what to do. He watched her as she ran across the parking lot and entered the building.

Fifteen minutes later, Kim was speed walking out of the hotel with Tyler on her hip. She got in the car almost out of breath.

"He's in room 216."

Damar didn't reply. He just started the car and drove off. He went a mile down the highway and pulled into a dollar store.

Before he got out of the car he turned to Kim with a smirk on his face. "Shawty, you ain't gonna ride off in my shit are you?"

Kim giggled and shook her head. "No, I can't even drive."

"To be on the safe side, I'm taking the keys," he said and hopped out of the car and ran into the store.

When Damar returned to the car, they both sat up straight and eye balled him. Damar had a big yellow bag in his hand. He reached inside and took out a Mountain Dew and a bag of potato chips, and then handed them to Kim. Then he got back on the highway and drove back to the hotel. Per his request, he got a room on the second floor, same as Detective Goldman.

Hours had passed since Damar had checked into the room. He had changed into a pair of jeans and a black long sleeve shirt that he grabbed at the dollar store to cover his tattoos on his arm. Kim and Tyler were asleep on the twin bed.

At precisely 10 p.m., Damar took the items he bought at the dollar store out of the bag and put them in his pocket. Then he threw on a pullover poncho and eased out of the room.

Detective Goldman's room was ten doors down and across the hall. There was one camera at the floor's exit. Damar walked under it, pulled out some grey tape, and put a piece of it over the lens. Then he went and knocked on his door. He responded after the third knock.

"Who is it?" he yelled from behind the door as he peered through the peep hole. He saw someone in a blue poncho with the hood hanging over his face. "What do you want?" Detective Goldman asked.

Damar held up the yellow bag and in a low tone, he said, "Extra towels."

The detective looked through the peep hole and saw that it was a black man. He became suspicious because the man was wearing a rain coat and the night sky was clear. So he slowly grabbed his gun from his shoulder holster. He carefully unlocked the door and slung it open with his gun behind his back.

Damar remained calm as creek water as the detective gave him a quizzical look. "I didn't call for any room service."

Damar pointed. "That lady over there said to give these to you."

Detective Goldman like a fool stuck his blonde head out the room and looked to his right.

Whoop!

That was the sound of the master lock mashing his temple. The detective's eyes rolled to the back of his head as he fell on his back. He was out cold.

Damar stepped in and secured the door, and then he looked down at Detective Goldman lying on the floor. He bent down and peeled his fingers off of the gun and placed it in his waist. Next, he dragged Detective Goldman in front of the dresser in the middle of the room and grabbed a chair. He then hoisted the detective up and sat him in it. The dead weight of his limp body proved to be a struggle keeping him upright, but eventually Damar secured him nice and tight with the duct tape he'd bought.

Once he was sure Detective Goldman was bound, he pulled out a box cutter, opened his mouth, grabbed his tongue and cut it. The intense pain shocked him back to consciousness.

His eyes popped open and he belted out a scream that sounded like a duck call, "Aha, aha, aha."

He tried to break free from his bondage, but failed.

Damar stood up and watched as blood poured from his mouth. Within seconds, his entire front was saturated with blood, and his body started to tremble as he was going into shock.

"Yeah, mutha'fucka, how does it feel when the rabbit got the gun? Huh? Huh? I can't hear you," Damar got up in his face.

The detective's eyes darted back and forth. He was oblivious to what the fuck was going on.

Damar chuckled and whispered in his ear, "It's the King, mutha'fucka." Then he looked Detective Goldman square in the eyes and lowered his eyebrows. "You made me change my life and my face and now I'm finna change your face, bitch."

Damar grabbed him by the hair and started cutting a circle around his face.

"Ahh, ahh, ahh," Goldman cried out as his eyes almost escaped their sockets.

Damar wasn't done, though. He wanted the detective to suffer and endure everything he put him and his family through. He wanted him to bleed to death and feel every drop of his blood running out of his body, like the pig he was. Damar dropped the razor and stuck his hand under a fold of skin by Goldman's jaw. He then began peeling his face off.

Halfway through the process, Damar decided to speed things up. He reached down and grabbed the box cutter and started cutting the rest of his skin off. When he was done, he stood and looked down at his masterpiece. The skin on Goldman's face was hanging on by the gristle in his nose and it looked like he had on a Halloween mask. Damar shifted to the side so Goldman could view his self in the mirror.

"How you like your new face, mutha'fucka?" Damar's adrenaline had him breathing heavily.

Goldman was far too weak to respond. He had lost too much blood and his head rolled from side to side. He was minutes away from the grim reaper coming to collect his soul.

For all the months you spent trying to bring me down, separating me from my mom, putting my girl in hiding, making me move from my home and keeping me from the world, this is payback, bitch! Damar thought.

Suddenly Detective Goldman's phone rung and broke Damar out of the sick state of mind he had put him in. Damar glanced at his watch. A half an hour had passed. He had stayed longer then he intended, but something came over him as soon as he laid eyes on the dirty detective.

Now he was staring at the aftermath of what he just did to a mutha'fucka that didn't know when to quit. Damar turned and started for the door because death was inevitable for Detective Goldman. As he reached for the doorknob, he thought about the last time he left a job unfinished. So he turned around and walked up behind him and snatched him by his drenched hair. He pulled his head back and rammed his blade into his windpipe and ripped it wide open. As Damar brought the blade back to his side, blood skeeted from the Detective's throat. He then put his wallet in his pocket. Then he put his hood back on his head and carefully exited the room.

Chapter 3

That night, Damar bleached the room down and left the hotel before sunrise. Detective Goldman's room door was still shut and that was a good thing. It meant housekeeping didn't start their shift yet and nobody had found the body.

On the way to *Hartsville Jackson International Airport* Damar made one stop at McDonalds to get them some breakfast. Next, they flew first class to *Jacksonville International Airport*. Two hours later, they were in a cab heading to Orange Park Subdivision where Kim's parents lived on Kingsley Avenue.

Damar could tell they were getting close to the house because Kim looked nervous and couldn't sit still. He gently tapped her on the shoulder.

"Yeah," she said.

Damar gave her a warm smile. "You gonna be a'ight, shawty?"

Kim smiled and leaned over and kissed Tyler on top of his head. As soon as she looked up, she saw the house just ahead. She covered her mouth and turned to Damar.

"What am I supposed to say?"

Damar reached over and placed his hand on Tyler's head.

"When they see lil man here, you ain't gonna have to say nothing, trust me."

"The house with the brick mailbox," Kim said to the cab driver as he was about to pass it.

He pulled over to the curb and parked.

Kim's dad was in the driveway washing his truck. He was a middle aged, dark skinned man with a husky build. He had a rugged look about him. Damar could tell he'd been working hard all his life.

Kim slowly stepped out of the car and put Tyler on her hip. Damar got out as well and walked around to her side. He handed her two hundred dollars, and she put it in her front pocket.

Then she looked up at Damar. "Thank you, Carl. I'll never forget you or what you've done for me."

Her appreciation made Damar smile. He wrapped his arms around her and Tyler and gave them a hug.

Kim's father turned around and curiously looked at the woman he didn't recognize as his daughter hugging a man off to the side of his driveway.

After a farewell hug, Damar lifted her chin. "Go on and I'll wait right here."

Kim tightened her lips and smiled. She slowly walked towards the house. Tyler waved at Damar as his mother carried him up the driveway. Damar threw up the deuces and leaned up against the cab.

"Kim, is that you?" her father asked.

"Yes, daddy, it's me, and this is my son Tyler. He's two. Daddy can I come..."

Before Kim could get it out of her mouth, her father reached out and gave her and Tyler a warm, welcoming hug.

"Oh, oh, my baby girl. Oh God, oh thank you Jesus, my baby girl is home," he praised, and then he stood upright with tears running down his face. "I had given up hope and I thought I'd never see you again.

Kim's mother had just stepped on the porch. She was bringing Kim's father something to drink. As soon as she laid eyes on the young lady, she knew who she was. She dropped everything she had in her hands and ran over.

After the three hugged and cried a spell, Kim thought about Carl.

She broke from her parents embrace. "Mom and dad I want y'all to meet somebody."

Then she turned to where the cab was parked and it was gone.

***

Thirty minutes later...

Damar was back on Hwy 15 heading to the airport to catch his flight to Miami. While en route, he tossed his cell phone out the window. A couple of hours later he was back at his mansion. When he opened the double doors, the first thing he saw was Boo Boo kicked back on his white leather sofa talking on the phone. Damar walked over and snatched the phone out of Boo Boo's hand.

Not knowing who took his phone, Boo Boo jumped up. "What the fuck?"

He relaxed once he saw it was Damar.

"Shhhh," Damar said, putting his finger to his lips. "Phone tapped," he whispered.

Boo Boo's mouth went into an O shape as he looked down at his phone in Damar's hands.

Damar went into the guest bathroom, broke the phone in half, and then he flushed it down the toilet. Boo Boo was standing in the doorway as his phone swirled down the drain. "What's up?" Boo Boo asked."

Damar looked up. "I'll tell you later. Where's my baby?"

"She's upstairs sleep. I checked on her about an hour ago," Boo Boo told him.

"Aight, where's Dub and Fresh?"

"Dub out by the pool and Fresh flew back to Georgia." Boo Boo replied.

Damar walked past him and straight to the pool.

Dub Sac was lying down on a beach chair by the Olympic sized pool with cocaine residue on his nose. He didn't know Damar and Boo Boo were standing over him.

Boo Boo noticed Dub Sac's powdery nose and glanced over at Damar who he could tell was hotter than fish grease.

"Dub," Damar yelled and instantly Dub Sac sprung to his feet.

Damar looked at him from head to toe. He had bags under his eyes like he'd been up all night.

"Hey, what's up, bruh? I see you done made it back. Yeah, me and Boo Boo held shit down fa' ya," he stuttered.

"When did you get back on the that shit?" Damar asked, rubbing his hands together.

Dub Sac dropped his head. "To tell you the truth, bruh, I ain't never quit. But you know it don't control me. Shit keeps me on point."

Damar sighed then looked out to his pool at the sparkling water.

"You know what Dub, I ain't even mad at cha. I'ma put it to you like this. The first time you fuck up with me and mines or cause me to lose something, I swear on my mama, Patricia, I'ma dead dock yo' ass. Compendia?"

Dub Sac slowly shook his head. "Bruh, I ain't gonna fuck up. That's something you ain't never got to worry about. I'll die before I let you go down."

"I'll remember that," Damar said.

Boo Boo looked at Damar sideways because he let Dub Sac off so easily. He was expecting Damar to snap.

Damar then reached out and told Dub Sac, "Let me see ya phone."

Dub Sac went in his front pocket and handed it to him.

"That bitch ass Detective Goldman showed up at mama's funeral. I think my line was tapped. That's the only thing I can see. So we just gonna get rid of all our phones. I got some phones on the way and we just gotta watch what we say over the phone. I'ma hit Fresh up real quick, and after this, we ain't using these phones again. "

Damar punched in Fresh's number and waited for the phone to ring.

Chapter 4

Fresh was banging Cassie from the back when his phone rang over on the nightstand. He ignored it and kept pumping her small hole. She had that snap back pussy and he wasn't letting up on it for nothing or no one. This was one of many delights that Fresh loved about her. Plus, she had a head game that could make a nigga toenails pop off.

"Huh, huh, oh yeah, baby. Oh shit yeah, baby. Oh shit yeah. You like dis dick, don't cha?" Fresh asked her as he watched his long cum coated pole slide in and out of her.

Fresh had been taming the pussy for the last thirty minutes. They started in the kitchen on the countertop. Then he carried her to the bedroom, so he could really beat her back out.

"Yesss, yes, daddy. Oh God, it feels so good. Fuck me, baby," Cassie begged with her ass in the air and her head sideways pressed against the pillow.

She was really stroking his ego and Fresh started going faster. You could see the veins in his arms and neck protrude as he tried his best to run his dick up through her esophagus. Sweat from his face dripped on her ass.

"Ahhh, ahhh. Ugh," he grunted with each doggy thrust.

"Ohhh my God. Ohhh shiiit. Ohhh, ohhh, I'm cumming," Cassie yelled as she dug her fingernails into the pillow.

Then she busted the biggest orgasm ever.

Her pussy felt so good and sloppy that it made Fresh swear, "Goddamn, oh shiiit! Mutha'fucka."

At that moment, this white bitch had the best pussy in the world. After Cassie got hers she decided to cheer him on so he could bust one.

"C'mon, baby. Give it to me. Give me that dick. Ohhh yes, like that," she said, while throwing her ass back.

"Here I cum, baby. Oh yeah, huh. Huh, ahhh," Fresh yelled as he took one final thrust that made Cassie scream.

Then his phone started ringing again. This time he was willing to answer it being that he was more than satisfied. He slowly pulled out of Cassie and smacked her on the ass. Then he walked over to the nightstand and answered his phone.

"Yeah, what's up, cuzo?" Fresh asked, breathing heavily into the phone.

"Whatever you got going on, you need to cut that shit short. You know where I'm at. Be here before midnight. Oh, and one more thing, pick up another car ASAP," Damar said talking in code. Fresh knew that meant to ditch the phone.

"Damn," Fresh said, rubbing his bald head.

Then he sat his phone back on the dresser and sat on the bed.

Cassie was now lying on her back with her legs wide open and she was playing in her pussy.

"Ummm, I'm so wet," she said, seductively.

Fresh's dick slowly rose to the occasion when he saw how wet her fingers were. *Shit, five more minutes won't hurt,* he thought t o himself before climbing on top of her and busting one last nut for the road.

In three minutes tops, Fresh was sliding out of Cassie once again. He rolled over and got out of bed and started putting his clothes on.

"What the fuck? Where are you going?" Cassie sat up.

Fresh didn't answer until he had his pants and shoes on.

"Baby, I'm sorry, but I gotta fly back to Miami."

"Aww, but you just got here. I miss you," Cassie confessed as she poked her lip out and crossed her arms.

Fresh sat down beside her and kissed her on the lips.

Then he said with a sincere look on his face, "I miss you, too, baby, but this is business."

Cassie moved him out of the way and went into the bathroom. Fresh followed her and stood in the door.

"So you mad now?" he asked.

Cassie grabbed her toothbrush and squeezed a dab of Colgate on it.

She turned to him. "If I knew this was going to happen, I wouldn't have taken my vacation."

Then she started brushing her teeth.

"Cassie, baby," Fresh said, getting agitated.

When she didn't pay him no mind and continued brushing her teeth, Fresh raised his voice to get her attention.

"*Cassie.*"

She stopped what she was doing and looked at him through the mirror with a frown on her pretty face. The sparkle in her eyes wasn't there anymore.

"Can't you see I'm brushing my teeth?" she asked.

"Them bitches white enough," Fresh said, and pulled her to him. Then he added. "Listen. Check this out. How about you come to Miami with me. That way I can introduce you to my cousin Damar and his fiancée," Fresh finally said and smiled.

Cassie damn near choked to death as she quickly turned and spit the toothpaste out of her mouth and into the sink.

"Baby, you alright?" Fresh asked as he patted her on the back.

Cassie coughed a little more before pulling herself together and splashing cold water on her face.

"Oh my God," she said as she reached for a towel.

Fresh pulled a pink one off the rack and handed it to her. Cassie thanked him and dried her face off.

"So what's up? You coming with me or what?" Fresh asked and slapped her on the ass.

Cassie forced a smile and pushed passed him. She went into the bedroom.

"Feels like I'm talking to myself." Fresh mumbled. "Say, what's up? Are you going?" he asked for the second time, while standing behind her as she started to make the bed.

She quickly spun around. "No."

"And why not? You ain't got shit else to do."

"Why? For one, when I ask you to come with me to my parents' house you always say, *Naw, I'm good. I'm good.*" She mocked him.

"But that's different, my cousin ain't like your folks. Yo' daddy is prejudice as fuck. I been done knocked his punk ass out," Fresh said, holding up a fist.

Cassie snapped her head up and looked at him in awe.

"That is not true. My dad is not like that. What would make you even think that?"

"Whatever, you just don't see it, but I do," Fresh said, and then picked his shirt off the floor and slipped it on.

Then he grabbed his phone and the keys to his rental car off the dresser. He walked back over to Cassie and took her by the waist.

"Yo, when I get back, I'ma go with you to your parent's house. So next time you won't have any excuses, a'ight," Fresh said, with a stern look on his face.

Cassie knew she had stepped in a pile of shit on this one. If she agreed to his terms she would have to tell him about her previous relationship with Damar. Then she would have to call Damar and explain this shady shit to him.

If she didn't agree, Fresh might get a bit suspicious about something. She quickly chose the former because she knew somewhere down the line it would come out.

"Okay, it's a deal," she said, giving him a fake smile.

Fresh smiled then he leaned over and gave her a juicy tongue kiss.

Muah.

"I'ma call you when I get to the airport, alright baby."

"Okay, be safe."

Frank Gresham

Chapter 5

After Damar got off the phone with Fresh he went and flushed Dub Sac's phone down the toilet. Then he went upstairs to surprise Jamerica. She wasn't expecting him until later. Jamerica was under the covers balled up like a baby when Damar entered their special bedroom. He slipped out of his socks and shoes in order to walk on the white carpet. He tipped over to the king size bed that had a leopard print canopy on it. He peeled the covers back slowly revealing his girl's flawless naked body. The chill from the brass ceiling fan woke her. When she saw Damar standing there, a smile appeared on her face. She was so happy to see her handsome man, but not too thrilled about getting a chill.

"If you're not going to put the covers back on me, you better get on top of me and keep me warm," she said, playfully.

Damar quickly stripped down to nothing.

He said with a grin on his face, "I ain't got no problem with that, shawty."

Then he climbed in the bed next to her. It was like a magnetic pull as their lips and hands connected.

They kissed passionately for a moment then Jamerica broke from his lips. "Damn, I missed your ass."

Damar ran his hand across her ripe nipple. "Not as bad as I missed you, baby."

He stole a couple of neck shots before she could start up a conversation. That was all it took for her to forget about the questions she wanted to ask him. She started moaning and threw her head back like he was Dracula and she was ready to be bitten.

"Oh baby," she moaned as she cradled the back of his head.

Damar snailed his tongue over her smooth collarbone. She cringed because it tickled and gave her the chills. Then he eased his hand down between her legs and started playing with her clit.

Seeing that she was already wet as a duck's ass, he propped one of her legs up and popped two fingers in her hole. He twirled them around until they were soaking wet. Then he got on top, slid down, and began cat licking her pussy. Jamerica hiked her legs up and grabbed his head with both hands.

"Ahhh, ahhh. Oh yeah, baby. Whoa, shit. Eat yo' pussy, baby. Eat dat shit."

It turned her on more watching Damar take his sweet time eating her out. He licked slowly and gently, and then suddenly she felt like she had to pee. She knew it was an orgasm about to come at any moment.

"Oh shit, baby. Oh shit, oh shit," she yelled, with her mouth wide open.

Damar knew what time it was so he rose up and got on his knees. He grabbed his hard dick and started smacking the head of it on her clit.

"Whoa, don't play wit' me, baby. Fuck me. Fuck me, please," she begged, shaking her head.

Damar gave her a crooked smile, and then he navigated his dick downward and slid in. He was going too slow for Jamerica so she lifted her ass and her pussy sucked the dick in. Her warm wetness sent chills up Damar's spine and the tight fit was perfect.

"Damn, baby, I see you ain't the only one who missed a nigga," he said, looking down at her rose pink lips fold in and out.

She had his thick chocolate pipe shining like Armoral tires. Jamerica continued to meet his anxious thrust and she knew this orgasm was going to be a mutha'fuckin' tsunami.

"Beat it, baby, beat dis pussy up," she demanded. "Beat it, ahhh, ahhh, fuck."

Damar arched his back and started jack hammering the pussy.

"Ugh, ugh, ugh," he grunted as he gyrated his hips.

Jamerica felt the tidal wave rushing and strangled the bed sheets.

"Oh, Damar. Oh my, oh, oh, oh, shiiit. Ahhh," she cried as she candy coated every inch of him.

Seconds after she came something serious, Damar felt his sperm flowing up through his shaft. He made an ugly face and started to jack off. Thick cum shot out of him like a rocket and landed on her stomach.

"Ahhh, ahhh, ahhh, ahhh," was all he could say.

***

Thursday Morning, Athens GA

A housekeeper walked into Detective Goldman's room a little after check out time to clean. As soon as she saw the faceless man bound to the chair she screamed and fainted in the doorway. An Asian man stepped out of his room and saw her laid out and the dead detective. He quickly dialed 911, and within the hour, the whole floor was taped off with yellow tape. Law enforcement, CSI agents, and paramedics were all crammed in the room. They had never seen a homicide like this before in all of Clarke County history. So the captain of the police force contacted the Feds.

As soon as the paramedics pronounced the unidentified man D.O.A, they were asked to step out while forensics did their job.

While every possible piece of evidence was being tagged and bagged, a huge black mutha'fuckathat had a permanent frown on his face walked in wearing a pair of jeans, sneakers, and a navy blue Nautica shirt. He was Detective Fred *Badass* Brown.

Fred was a hardcore dignified brother. His movements, his speech, and demeanor all whispered, *Respect me*. He'd been working for the feds going on twenty years. He was dedicated, determined, and dependable to his job just like channel five news. It didn't matter if he knew the victim or not. He made every case in his district personal.

He walked over to the victim and motioned for the forensic person that was digging under Detective Goldman's fingernail to move out the way so he could quickly examine the body. He rubbed his chin as he walked around the chair.

He assumed that this homicide was personal and that they had a serial killer in Athens who was trying to make a statement.

He then looked around the room and saw no forced entry and no sign of a struggle.

After his final conclusion, he asked, "So who was he?"

A white rookie detective with a buzz cut, wearing a white shirt and brown khakis, stepped to Detective Brown. "The room was checked in by Federal Agent Richard Goldman from Lexington, Kentucky. He's a white male, forty-seven years of age, married with two kids, and he was a fifteen-year veteran, sir."

Fred glanced back down at the body. "Shit, what business did he have here in Georgia?"

"He was tracking down a dangerous drug lord by the name of Damar Val King."

Fred rubbed his chin. "Ummm King, I need to see the surveillance cameras now."

Chapter 6

In Miami the sun was rising, and it looked like it was coming out of the ocean. Damar was chilling on the balcony and staring up at the seagulls as they flew freely without a care in the world. He glanced through the French doors at Jamerica lying on the bed all snuggly. A smile came across his face when he thought about his seed growing inside of her. He peered back out to the sea and closed his eyes. As the ocean breeze kissed his face, he had a quick epiphany of him and Jamerica flying high in the sky like a pair of white doves until the doorbell chimed and killed his daydream.

He left the balcony and grabbed his purple robe from the closet. He trotted down the stairs as he slipped his robe on. He walked to the front door and looked through the peep hole. Fresh was standing there crisp and clean in an all white Stacey Adams linen suit with his hat tilted to the side.

"You're late, nigga," Damar said as he opened the door.

Fresh grinned and threw his hands up all cool. "Yo, cuzo, blame it on the airport. You know they checking temperatures and all for that Ebola bullshit."

Then he stepped on in the house.

"Yeah, I know," Damar replied, and closed the door behind him.

As the two walked towards the kitchen, Damar asked, "Hey, did you get rid of your phone?"

"Yeah, cuzo, I always do what you tell me to do," Fresh said as they entered the kitchen.

"Cool, I sent an email to my IBM guy last night to bring me some new ones pronto," Damar explained, while opening the refrigerator and taking out a carton of pineapple juice. After he poured a glass he continued, "I think the feds had my phone tapped."

"Why you say that?" Fresh asked, grabbing him a seat at the table.

Damar almost gave Fresh a recount of his last forty-eight hours, but he decided not to. Even though he trusted his cousin with his life, some things were just better untold. He didn't want Fresh to think that he was beyond crazy if he knew how he rearranged Detective Goldman's face.

"Say, cuz, why you say that?" Fresh asked again, seeing Damar was in deep thought about something.

Damar snapped out of his trace, took a swallow of his juice, and then said, "I just figured it's time to switch up, that's all. Besides, good things only last for so long you know."

"Yeah, you right, cuz." Fresh agreed, then he asked, "Where's Dub Sac and Boo Boo?"

Damar got up and placed the juice carton back in the refrigerator. He started walking towards the living room. He stopped at the kitchen door.

"I don't know, but I'm 'bout to wake they asses up."

Damar went and sat at Jamerica's piano and started pounding on the keys.

Bun, Bun, Bun. Bun, Bun, Bun, Bun, Bun, Bun, Bun, Bun, Bun.

Boo Boo was the first one to pop up from the den. Then Dub Sac came out of the guest room. Jamerica was at the top of the steps looking over the rail just as Fresh was dapping in the room.

Once everyone was up and present, Damar stood up from the piano. "Everyone in my office now, this is an emergency meeting."

He then walked towards his office. Jamerica started down the steps, while rubbing her eyes.

"Not you," Damar said to his girl, and proceeded to his office.

"Good," Jamerica said, and went back to their bedroom.

When they got to his office, Damar sat behind his black marble top desk. Fresh sat on the black recliner, and Boo Boo and Dub

Sac sat on the black sofa. Damar noticed his surveillance cameras were showing static.

"Yo, Boo Boo, what's up? Why my cameras ain't working?"

"They were working this morning. I'ma go check the line."

"Hold up, you can fix that after the meeting," Damar said.

Damar's office was huge and was decorated just the way he liked it. The floors were Italian marble and the walls were decorated with pictures of celebrities and icons that he had meet some place or another. Behind him was a large picture of Tupac and the Outlaws taken from the *Hit 'em Up* video shoot. A life size poster of Michael Jordan doing the dunk he was most noted for, flying from the free throw line was to the right of him by the window. Among his many pictures, those two were his favorite.

While everyone sat patiently to see what the meeting was about, Damar opened his laptop and sent an email to Taz telling him to get rid of his phone and to relay the message to Oga and Lucky who were also in the rig with him transporting his product. Then he asked what their location was. Taz emailed back to let him know it was okay about the phone and that they were dropping the last truck load of coke off in Cocoa Beach, and then they were heading back to the warehouse to re-up.

Damar replied back and told him to let him know when they touchdown in Miami. He said he would meet them at the warehouse and then pressed send. Damar pushed the laptop to the side and took a big stretch.

"Ahhh," he said, and placed his elbows on the desk. He rubbed his palms over his face. He sighed. "Gava called me on my flight to Georgia."

At the mention of Gava's name, everybody became more attentive.

"What that nigga talking about, cuz?" Fresh asked, seeing Damar's jaw muscles bulging and the look on his face like the mention of Gava's name tasted like shit.

Damar sucked his teeth. "He wants thirty percent of our profit here in Miami."

Now everyone felt a little of what Damar was feeling. It killed Dub Sac's high and Boo Boo slammed his fist into his palm. Fresh just shook his head.

"Just when things were going smooth, Gava pulls some shit like this," Fresh said.

"So what you tell him?" Dub Sac asked with that killer mug on his face.

"I told that nigga to suck my mutha'fuckin' dick. Then I hung up on him. That's what I told him. So y'all know what this could mean," Damar stated.

"Hee, hee, hee, war time, baby," Dub Sac laughed, while rubbing his hands together.

"Yeah, Dub, I know he's coming, but the question is when," Damar said.

"When?" We gonna wait around like sitting ducks?" Boo Boo stood, and then he went on to say, "Bruh, Gava don't know you like we know you. He gonna come for our nuts with no hesitation."

"When he makes that mistake and thinks this shit is soft as cotton, there's gonna be a lot of body bags. And they ain't gonna be ours," Damar stated.

"You got that shit right," Dub Sac said.

"A'ight cuz so what about Taz and them?" Fresh asked.

"What about 'em?" Damar asked, raising an eyebrow.

"Shit, they Jamaican, too. For all we know, they could be in with Gava," Fresh said, clarifying the reason for his question.

"Naw, I don't think so, Fresh. They true Jamaicans and Gava some real bullshit. I doubt they fuck with him on that level, but I'm not saying I ain't gonna keep my eyes on 'em. I blame myself. This greedy shit didn't escalate until I started buying kilos by the truckload from that nigga, and then he jacked the prices up. That was my sign right there to quit fucking with his bitch ass. In the meantime, I want y'all to stay here. That way nobody gets caught slipping."

"Damar, bruh, I promised Shonda I was coming home as soon as you got back," Boo Boo said.

"Naw, you better send her ass a plane ticket. I meant what I said," Damar said, seriously.

"A'ight, I got cha," Boo Boo said with disappointment.

"Dub and Fresh, y'all good?" Damar asked.

"Shit, I'm good, like pork chops on white bread my nigga. I ain't got hoe problems. Hee, hee, hee," Dub Sac said, looking over to Fresh and Boo Boo with a smirk on his face.

Suddenly, an e-mail notification popped up on Damar's screen. It was a message from Mark, his IBM technician. The message read: *Hey, I'm outside.*

Damar zig zagged the screen with his finger and typed in, *come in.* He then spun around and got up to walked over to the intercom system mounted in the wall. It was channeled to the main parts of the house. He pressed a button and spoke into the speaker.

"Hey, baby, wake up. Come down to my office and bring your phone."

Jamerica was already up getting dressed to go to her doctor's appointment that she forgot to tell Damar about. Damar walked back to his desk and sat down.

"Hey, Boo Boo, go and let Mark in," Damar instructed as he leaned back in his chair and laced his fingers together.

Frank Gresham

Chapter 7

Boo Boo was leading Mark into the office. Mark was one of them cool ass white boys and smart as fuck. He stood a slim six feet tall with brown hair, and he dressed like a hippie. Damar's brother Mario had put him on to Mark just shortly before he was murdered.

Damar tested his loyalty several times before he was able to trust him by sending other dealers to him to try and purchase some of his high tech radio cell phones. On each occasion, no matter how tough they came at him or how much they offered to spend, he didn't fold.

"Yo, yo, what's good money?" Mark asked, reaching over to shake Damar's hand.

Damar dapped him up. "Shiiit, everything until somebody try to get over on ya, and then shit turn sour. Ya feel me?"

"Yeah, I feel ya man. That's why when somebody fuck with me, I get on my laptop and zap there fucking credit to shit," Mark said with a lot of head and hand motion.

Damar smiled at Mark's animation. "I'll be sure not to fuck you over, Mark. Let me see what you got for me."

Mark took the brown leather bag off his shoulder and sat it down. He unzipped it and placed eight radio phones on the desk. As soon as he did, Jamerica came in the room and brought her sweet perfume with her. She waved to everyone and sauntered over to Damar. She sat on his lap and wrapped her arms around his neck.

"Good morning, my king," she said, and kissed him on the lips. *Muah. Muah.*

"Morning, baby, and how did you sleep?" he asked, while rubbing her back and licking her peach lip gloss off his lips.

Jamerica smiled, put her hand on her stomach, and then said, "Me and the baby slept real good."

Every head in the room turned. They didn't know she was pregnant, she wasn't showing.

"Baby?" Boo Boo asked as he bucked his eyes.

"You joking, right?" Fresh then asked, sitting up in the recliner.

Jamerica looked at Damar and tilted her head.

"They don't know?" she asked surprised.

"Baby, it's been so much going on I forgot," Damar said.

"That's what's up, cuzo, and congratulations," Fresh said, holding up two thumbs.

Jamerica cleared her throat and stuck out her left hand for everyone to see the diamond ring on her finger.

"Don't you have something else to tell them?" she asked, batting her eyelashes.

When they all noticed the sparkling rock, Damar didn't have to tell them anything. Everyone except Dub Sac started clapping and cheering. When the room quieted down, Dub Sac put his two cents in.

"I ain't getting married and I ain't having no kids either. Hee, hee, hee, but congrats, my nigga."

"'Preciate it, fellas, y'all grab a phone," Damar said, and kissed Jamerica again.

While his crew was turning on their new phones, Damar turned and asked Jamerica where she was going all dolled up. Her hair was in a classic updo style and she was wearing a baby blue and white sundress with white sandals.

"Oh, oh, that's what I forgot to tell you, baby. We have a doctor's appointment at ten today."

"Oh, we do, do we?" Damar asked, teasing her. He then looked at his watch and noticed it was 9:25 a.m. "Shit, I need to be getting in the shower. Let me see your phone real quick, baby." Jamerica politely handed Damar her phone. "Do you know all your important numbers off the top of your head?" Damar asked, while examining her phone.

"Yeah, baby, why?" she asked, while rubbing the back of his neck.

"'Cause you gotta get rid of your phone, too. Hey, Boo Boo, flush this bitch down the toilet."

He handed him the phone. Boo Boo took the phone, headed towards the office bathroom, and flushed it.

"Since you just flushed my five hundred dollar phone and insist that I use that ugly whatever that is," Jamerica said, pointing to the phone on the desk, "Can you at least tell me why?"

"I think our phones were tapped. You remember the detective that tried to blackmail me? Well, he showed up at mama's funeral and I only remember making one call and that was to Uncle Henry. What really has me thinking is I can't figure out how did he know we had a house in Beverly Hills. Nobody knew about that spot but me and you. Anyway, grab a phone off the table and it's only to be used when you're calling me a'ight, baby?"

He programmed their phone with each other's number.

"But what about when I call my mama and Tamika?" Jamerica whined.

"Go buy another phone for that shit and don't tell anybody where we live. The same goes for y'all, too," Damar said, looking at his crew. "These phones are for communication with the cartel only and wiring all money transactions. Cop a prepaid phone for your personal dealings."

When they all nodded that they understood something popped up in Jamerica's head.

"Hey, baby, I just remembered, Tamika called me that night in L.A. Oh my God," she said, recalling what this might mean.

Damar looked at Jamerica sideways. "Did you tell her where you was at?"

Jamerica covered her mouth and just nodded yes. Damar gently rubbed her thigh.

"It's okay, baby, 'cause they had to find out another way. I don't think Tamika would do something like that," Damar said, and winked at Dub Sac.

"Hee, hee, hee," Dub Sac snickered.

Jamerica's head snapped up at Dub Sac then at Damar.

"No Damar," she said.

"What?"

Damar tried to sound innocent.

"You know what! Why that ugly mutha'fucka over there laughing and shit," Jamerica said, pointing at Dub Sac.

"Well that's my cue 'cause I gotta go," Mark said. He knew it was time to go. He didn't want to be a witness to nothing. "I hate to run, money, but I have to get back to Atlanta."

Mark threw his bag over his shoulder, and then saw himself out of the office.

"A'ight, 'preciate it, Mark, peace. Ah yo, Boo Boo, walk him to the door," Damar said, after throwing up the peace sign.

"Yo, I'm good, money. I don't need an escort. Peace y'all," Mark said, and left in a hurry.

Jamerica was still upset about Dub Sac snickering. She was still sitting on Damar's lap with her lip poked out. She knew that Damar had given him some kind of signal to get at Tamika.

She looked Damar in his eyes. "Are you going to kill Tamika?"

Damar couldn't lie to her. At least not to her face so he just ignored the question. He went to doodling with his laptop. Jamerica reached over and closed it.

Then she grabbed his chin. "Answer me, Damar."

He frowned and opened his laptop back up.

"Girl, you better quit playing. You know I ain't got no sympathy for no mutha'fuckin' snitch."

Jamerica grabbed her face and started crying. Damar went to hold her, but she broke from his grasp and ran out of the office.

Damar shook his head. "Women."

Fresh stepped to Damar, propped against the desk, and whispered so the others couldn't hear, "Ayo, cuzo, I need to holla at you for a minute on some personal shit. Me and my girl made a deal, right. The only way she's coming to Miami is if I meet her parents."

"So what you saying is that you gotta fly back to Georgia," Damar cut his eyes at him.

"Yeah, cuz, I'm just going to introduce myself, and then me and my girl we're out."

Damar rubbed his temple and thought, S*hit, won't be right if I let him go and not Boo Boo.*

"A'ight, cuz, tell Boo Boo he can go, too. I want y'all back in forty-eight hours."

"That's what's up," Fresh said, and smiled, while giving Damar some dap.

Ka Boom! Boom!

Everyone dropped to the floor.

"What the fuck," Damar yelled as he squatted beside his desk looking around. "Y'all a'ight?"

"It came from outside," Fresh yelled, while down on the floor.

Damar grabbed his Glock from the desk drawer and at the same time everyone else was pulling out their guns.

Damar cocked his weapon and ran out of the office. His crew got up and followed.

Before they got to the front door, Damar turned to Boo Boo. "Watch Jamerica."

Boo Boo turned and hightailed it up the staircase. Damar, Fresh, and Dub Sac ran out the front door.

"Oh shiiit, mutha'fucka," Damar screamed, while waving his Glock in the air.

Fresh and Dub Sac were in awe and clutching their guns. They we're ready to bust at anything moving.

They looked on as Mark's blue Yukon was engulfed in flames and slowly coasting between the hedges.

"Quick, get the fire extinguishers," Damar yelled.

Fresh and Dub Sac ran into the four car garage that was separated from the house. Within seconds, they were putting out the blazing fire.

Damar ran over, mad as a raging bull, and watched. When there was nothing but grey smoke coming from the Yukon, Damar and his boys walked over to the driver's side and peeked inside the truck. They expected to see Mark's charred remains.

"What the fuck is this?" Fresh asked after seeing that the Yukon was empty.

They all looked at each other clueless as a mutha'fucka.

"Gava," Dub Sac said, and dropped the extinguisher. Then Fresh dropped his, too. At that moment, Damar took off running towards the house. The guys followed suit.

Chapter 8

Fresh and Dub Sac quickly went and started gathering their belongings. Damar scaled the stairs. When he topped the steps, Boo Boo was laid out on the floor with a gash in the back of his head. He instantly went into panic mode.

"Oh shit, Jamerica, Jamerica, Jamerica," Damar screamed as he rushed into his bedroom.

When he didn't see her there, he checked the walk-in closet, and then the other bedroom, and Jamerica was in neither.

Fresh and Dub Sac heard Damar cry out so they stopped what they were doing and ran upstairs. When Dub Sac saw Boo Boo on the floor leaking, he fell to his knees and checked his pulse.

"Boo Boo, Boo Boo," Dub Sac yelled, in fear that his longtime friend might be dead.

Fresh saw Damar coming out of another bedroom down the hall and he could see the fear in his eyes, even from a distance. With Boo Boo down it was easy to piece together what had happened.

"I'll go check downstairs, cuz," Fresh said. Before Fresh descended the stairs, he stopped and looked at Dub Sac. "Is he dead?"

Dub Sac looked up. "No, he's still breathing."

Fresh nodded then ran down the stairs. For thirty minutes he and Damar searched the huge house looking for Jamerica.

By this time, Boo Boo had come to and was now sitting on the floor with his back against the wall. Dub Sac was applying alcohol to his head wound when Damar walked up with his head down. He was weak and teary eyed. He felt like his soul had been snatched away from him. He came to a halt in the hallway and dropped to his knees. He closed his eyes and let the tears stream down his face. A few seconds later, Fresh walked up the hall and walked over and stood by Dub Sac and Boo Boo.

They all stared at their leader with his head down. Fresh wasn't sure if he was praying, so he didn't say anything. That's exactly what he was doing. He was praying to God that whoever took Jamerica wouldn't hurt her or his seed in any way. He was at God's mercy. He silently repented for killing so many people, and causing pain and grief to their families. He never felt this way before, not even with the death of his mother and brother. Jamerica was his soulmate and the pain squeezed at his heart. He promised her that he would protect her with his life. Instead, he slipped and let her be taken away.

Damar's crew remained quiet, while he sincerely spoke to God until a police siren broke the silence.

"Shit, the po po," Fresh said, and ran into the bedroom across from Damar's to look out the window.

He saw a squad car pulling in the driveway.

"One car, two pigs," Fresh yelled, as he saw them jumping out of the car.

Damar raised his head, took a deep breath, and then stood.

"I got this. Fresh, watch my back," Damar said, and went in his bedroom.

He put his Glock on the dresser, while he slipped on a pair of jeans and a T-shirt. Next he put his Glock in the small of his back and went into the hallway.

Damar calmly walked past Dub Sac and Boo Boo, and then trotted down the steps and out the front door. Two cops were standing next to the burnt Yukon. One was black as an ace of spades and chunky. He was snoopping around the vehicle. His leathery face showed that he was up in age. The white cop was slim and looked like he had just finished high school.

As Damar approached the rookie and the vet, Fresh's instincts kicked in. He opened up the bedroom window. He wasn't sure what Damar was up to, but he had his front and his back. Both cops placed their hands on their belts, elbows out, when Damar stopped in front of them.

"What happened here?" the black officer asked as he lowered his brows at Damar.

Damar looked at his name tag. "I don't know, Officer Reid. It might have been a gas leak or something. I was inside eating breakfast when I heard a big explosion," Damar said, holding back his real emotions.

The young cop, whose name was Officer Walker, bought Damar's story and just nodded. Officer Reid wasn't buying it. For one, the Yukon was not in a parking space. It was out of gear, he noticed. Meaning someone was in it at one point before it exploded. He then stepped closer to Damar and looked him over. Then he scanned the property. The landscaping was colorful and nicely manicured. The limos and the Bentley were extra clean. Damar had recently had them detailed. Jamerica's red convertible Audi was shining like a ruby red apple. The Rolls Royce is what really prompted the cop to ask Damar a question unrelated to why they were there.

"Is this your house?" Officer Reid asked.

Damar sighed, *Damn why they send this Uncle Tom ass nigga.* Damar knew where this was heading if he didn't finagle his answer carefully.

"Naw, it's a rental," Damar lied.

"Umm, so what do you do for a living Mr.Um—" The cop asked, trying to get a name.

"Carl Grant, I'm a stockbroker from New Mexico," Damar said.

Officer Reid then stuck his hand out. "Let me see your driver's license."

At this point Damar's virtue of patience was gone. Finding Jamerica was the only thing that mattered to him now and this house nigga was holding that process up.

"Look man, I ain't going through all that shit today. Nigga, I told you what happen," Damar said angily.

Damar checked Officer Reid in front of his partner, and that ticked him off. Now he didn't give a fuck who Damar was. All he knew was that he was young, black, rich, and most likely a drug dealer. So being the cocky mutha'fucka that he was, he decided to use a little force in getting Damar to cooperate.

"Okay, *smart ass,* since you got jokes, how about I lock your ass up just because I can?" Officer Reid said, and reached for Damar's wrist.

Damar jerked his arm away.

"Get your mutha'fuckin' hands off me."

The cop went for his gun, but Damar was quicker and grabbed his hand. They began to tussle. Officer Walker pulled out his mace can.

"No, don't spray him, you'll hit me, too. Use your baton," Officer Reid yelled.

Officer Walker whipped out his Billy club and struck Damar behind the knee repeatedly.

"Ahhh shit, you pussy mutha'fucka," Damar screamed, before pushing the black cop to the ground.

Then he turned and scooped Officer Walker up. He lifted him in the air and slammed him on the asphalt. By this time Fresh and Dub Sac were busting through the front door with their guns in hand. The impact of the body slam took the breath out of the rookie cop. Damar quickly jumped to his feet, but he was a second too late. Officer Reid already had his gun out and pointed at his chest. Damar froze and put his hands in the air, while breathing heavy.

"Here comes my boys mutha'fucka," Damar said with a smile.

Dub Sac and Fresh stopped a few feet away.

Fresh yelled out, "Drop it, mutha'fucka. Drop dat shit!"

Dub Sac countered, "You heard him. Drop it, nigga, before we light dat ass up."

"I'm a police officer. You drop yours," Officer Reid yelled back, while keeping his aim locked on Damar. "Drop it."

"Fuck dat, we'll all go to hell," Fresh said, gritting his teeth.

While the three were going back and forth, the rookie cop discreetly pulled his weapon and fired two wild shots at Fresh. He missed badly. Dub Sac was the first to return fire. He hit Officer Walker in his shoulder. Officer Reid spun around and got one shot off. Damar grabbed his Glock from his back and shot Officer Reid in the back of the head.

Bloww. Bloww.

The veteran dropped to the ground. Damar pointed at the rookie who was holding his shoulder and crying like a bitch.

"Ohhh, ohhh, ohhh," Officer Walker cried out.

"Try another occupation in the afterlife mutha'fucka," Damar said, and then shot him in the face.

Blocka!

Damar then limped over to Dub Sac and Fresh, while holding his leg

"Ahhh, ahhh, shit, that mutha'fucka tried to break my shit. Come on, we gotta get the fuck away from here and find Jamerica. Grab my laptop, set the house on fire, and then meet me in the limo."

"A'ight, cuzo. Let's go, Dub," Fresh said, and they ran to the garage and came back with two gas cans.

Damar took one and poured gas on his vehicles inside and out, and then set them ablaze. Fresh went inside and grabbed Damar's laptop, and then helped Boo Boo out to the limo. Dub Sac was dousing the house with gasoline. Damar sat behind the wheel with Fresh riding shot gun as they patiently waited on Dub Sac. Boo Boo was stretched out on the backseat holding an ice pack to his head. His leg was moving from side to side. Damar could tell he was in a lot of pain from looking at him through the rearview.

"Say, Boo Boo, you a'ight big homie?" Damar asked.

"Yeah, I'm good, bruh," Boo Boo replied.

You could hear the pain filter through his voice.

"What the fuck is taking Dub so long?" Fresh asked, looking over the dashboard.

No sooner than he said that Dub Sac was bolting out the door. He jumped off the porch and got in the backseat with Boo Boo. Damar then put the car in gear and punched it. He drove nonstop to the warehouse.

***

Taz and Oga were standing by the rig when Damar and the crew pulled up in the limo. Damar hopped out first, followed by his crew. The two Jamaicans could tell something was wrong by everyone's facial expressions.

"Gwan?" Oga greeted them with his raspy voice as Damar and the others approached the dock.

"Gava got Jamerica," Damar said as he ran up the ramp.

"Oh breda," Taz said, and grabbed a hold of his dreadlocks.

Damar went straight to the rear of the storage room. He felt his pocket for his keys.

"Shit," he said, frustrated.

He pulled out his Glock, and then shot the lock.

Blocka. Blocka.

He kicked the door open, and then he flipped the light switch on. He walked over to the gun case against the wall and opened it. He took out two 9mm's and loaded them before putting on his bulletproof vest. The crew followed suit.

After everyone was strapped up, Damar gave Taz and Oga their new phones. As they were making their way back to the front of the warehouse, Fresh walked up beside Damar.

"Ayo, cuzo, where we going? We don't know where to start looking."

"We going to every spot that mutha'fucka owns," Damar said.

"What if she's dead already?" Fresh asked Damar, whose eyes were blazing red.

Damar stopped in his tracks and grabbed Fresh by his shirt.

"Nigga, don't you ever say no shit like that ever again," Damar screamed.

Fresh flinched and held his breath for a split second until Damar turned him loose. Then they followed him out to the dock. Damar looked around his parking lot and pointed to his black van.

"Any gas in it?" he asked.

"Ya mon, it's full to the rim," Oga replied.

Damar then noticed Lucky wasn't present. He frowned and looked at Taz and Oga.

"Where the fuck is Lucky?"

Taz shrugged his shoulders and looked at Oga.

Damar turned to Oga. "Where that nigga at?"

"He left with his Boopsie," Oga said.

"What the hell is a Boopsie?" Damar questioned him.

"A woman well kept by a sugar daddy is a Boopsie," he explained.

Lucky's Boopsie was named Erica and she was from West Palm Beach. Damar remembered seeing her once about two weeks ago when she brought Lucky some lunch to the warehouse. He figured she had to tell Lucky something really good for him to leave his post after he was given a direct order.

"Fuck! I gotta find my girl. I'll deal with him later. Fresh, you drive," Damar said, and they all piled up in the van.

Frank Gresham

Chapter 9

Gava owned two Jamaican restaurants in Miami and one service station. The service station was on West 21st Street, which was closer, so they went there first. When they arrived at the service station Damar hopped out before Fresh could put the van in park. His crew stepped out one by one and followed him inside.

The doorbell made a loud clang when Damar pushed the door open. The customers at the counter turned around and the cashier stopped his change count. The clerk looked Jamaican. He had thick dreads, a nappy beard, and wore trendy clothes.

"Yo, son, you can't be busting in here like that," the clerk advised in a northern accent.

Damar didn't say a word. He just stormed towards the counter and shoved the two customers out the way. He reached over the counter and snatched the clerk by his locks. He pulled him across the countertop onto the floor.

"Aww, fuck, man, you buggin'," the clerk said, holding the top of his head.

"Nigga, shut the fuck up," Damar said, and kicked him in the ass.

"Ahh shiiit," the clerk cried out.

Now he was holding his head and his ass.

"Dub Sac, lock the door," Damar yelled over his shoulder.

Dub Sac went and secured the door, and then he closed the blinds.

"Oga, Taz, and Boo Boo, y'all go check the back," Damar ordered.

"Man, what you want? There ain't no money back there. It's all in the cash register," the clerk confessed.

Damar then snatched his gun from his waist. "Nigga, I ask the questions here, you don't."

Before he could get his first question out, a Korean woman in her mid forties became hysterical when she saw the chrome Glock in Damar's hand. She started jumping in place and calling the man upstairs.

"Oh my God! My God! Oh Lord!"

The next thing you know, the pint size woman's head exploded into a thousand pieces.

Splat!

When her body fell to the floor, Dub Sac was standing over her with a smoking 12 gauge.

"Hee, hee, hee. Anybody else wanna make a call?" Dub Sac asked, while waving the gun at the remaining customers who gathered closer together.

When no one said a word, Damar put his foot on the clerks head and applied pressure. The man automatically started kicking and screaming.

"Ahhh, ahhh. Ooh, ahhh," he wailed as the rest of Damar's crew rushed back up front after hearing the gun blast.

"Bomba clot," Taz said, looking down at the headless woman as he walked around her.

Boo Boo did a quick glance at the dead lady then threw his hands up at Damar.

"She ain't here," he said.

Oga and Taz shook their heads indicating that they agreed.

"Fuck," Damar said, and ran his hand down his face.

Fresh tapped him on the shoulder and pointed to the camera above the cash register.

"Look, cuzo," Fresh said, narrowing his eyes at the monitor.

Damar then kicked the clerk in the back.

"Ugh," the clerk cried out.

"Hey, mutha'fucka, where the tape at?" Damar asked.

"Ahhh, under the counter, yo," the clerk said, and rolled on his back.

"Boo Boo, grab the tape," Damar said, waving his gun.

Boo Boo swiftly ran behind the counter and found the tape. He brought it to Damar. Damar stuck it in his pocket, and then he cocked his Glock and pointed it at the clerk.

"Listen, mutha'fucka, you tell Gava if he don't get my girl back to me safely, I'ma kill everything from his grandma on down. Then I'm coming for his bitch ass."

"Man, I don't know nothing about no girl. I swear," the clerk said, shielding his face with his forearm.

Dub Sac then stepped beside Damar and aimed the 12 gauge at the man. "Dis nigga lying. Let me blow his fuckin' head off."

"Man, I just work here. I don't even know Gava," the man said.

Damar pushed Dub Sac's barrel away.

"Naw, we gonna let him live. If he's lying or not I'm pretty sure Gava will get the message," Damar said, and kicked the clerk again.

"Right, mutha'fucka," Damar yelled at him.

"Ahhh," the man moaned.

"C'mon, cuz. We wasting time here. We gotta go check the restaurants," Fresh suggested as he looked around.

"Hold up, let me kill the customers since we gonna let him live. One witness is better than four," Dub Sac said, walking up on them waving his gun.

Damar narrowed his eyes at them debating if he should let them live. They were innocent bystanders. One black man, a white couple, and one guy who looked mixed. Damar knew Dub Sac was right. These petrified patrons would grow some nuts behind a glass wall if they had him in a lineup.

"Let's ride, fellas," Damar said, and walked by Dub Sac. Then he whispered, "Wait till I leave."

Then he led the rest of the crew out to the van.

Once they got in the van, Fresh hit the switch and the V8 engine came alive. He looked over at Damar. The pain and fear was evident on his face. Even though he tried to hide it with his anger, it was still there. Fresh was blood and he could almost feel his cousin's pain if the others couldn't. He attempted to apologize for what he said about Jamerica being dead earlier. Then five shots echoed from inside the store.

Boom. Boom. Boom. Boom. Boom.

A few seconds later, Dub Sac came running out of the store and hopped in the van. Fresh then pulled back on the highway and headed to one of Gava's restaurants five miles from the service station.

When they got a mile up the road, Damar slid his phone out of his pocket and dialed Jamerica's number. It went straight to voicemail.

"Shit," Damar said, and tossed his phone on the floor board. He looked at Fresh. "Hey, cuz, if that mutha'fucka hurt Jamerica and my baby, I ain't gonna sleep until I kill him and his entire family. I swear to God."

Damar was missing Jamerica with a passion. He had never felt that way about anyone before. He found it hard to breath at times. *Baby girl, where are you?* He said to himself.

Fresh didn't want to see the pain in Damar's face so he just nodded, and then he glanced in his rearview mirror and saw blue lights.

"Oh shit 5.0," Fresh said, and started to punch it.

"Chill, chill, don't panic. Just pull over. I got this," Damar said, and snatched his banger from his waist.

Fresh flipped on his blinker and slowed down to pull over. The police car went around.

Zoom.

Fresh exhaled, and then pulled back into traffic.

Damar turned around and made eye contact with Dub Sac, who was sitting back on the seat looking like a ventriloquist dummy. He didn't say anything. He just stared at him.

"What? Hee, hee, hee," Dub Sac said, and held out his hands as if he didn't know why Damar was looking at him.

"Hee, hee, hell. I heard five shots back at the service station. There was only supposed to be four. I just thought I'd let you know." Damar then faced the front before Dub Sac could justify his actions.

Twenty minutes later, they pulled up to *The Coconut Hut*, one of Gava's restaurants. The place was a small blue building surrounded by palm trees. The eating area was outside and huge white umbrellas covered the tables. Fake flamingos were on the grass. Dub Sac was so anxious he went to step out the van with his gun in his hand.

"Hold up, Dub. They wouldn't bring her here. Yo, Taz, is Gava's other restaurant set up like this one?" Damar asked, while peeping the scene.

"Yeah, mon, exact same ting," Taz replied.

"Fuck," Damar yelled, smacking the dashboard.

"What else does Gava own around this mutha'fucka?" Dub Sac asked out loud.

Oga rubbed his chin and thought for a second.

Taz suddenly interrupted Oga's thoughts when he remembered one other spot Gava owned.

"Aha, he has a paint and body shop on Washington Ave." Taz yelled to the front of the van.

Fresh then programmed the GPS to the address.

"Got it," he said, when the map showed on the screen.

***

Once they reached Washington Avenue, Fresh drove a quarter of a mile before they saw the body shop on the left. It was a white building with a green tin roof. There was a large sign on top of it that said, *Gava's Paint & Body*.

When Fresh pulled into the lot, Damar told everyone to conceal their weapons. All six cartel members hopped out of the van looking like they meant business. Dub-Sac had a limp because he had the 12 gauge stuffed in his pants.

When the buzzer went off at the door, the man behind the desk looked up. He was a tall brother. He had to be every bit of 6'7" with a fade haircut. He was wearing a white shirt, red tie, and black slacks.

"Good morning gentleman, how can I help you?" the clerk asked with a practiced smile.

Damar walked right up to the counter and grabbed the guy by his tie. The man went to pry his hand away and Damar head butted him. His knees buckled. He braced himself on the counter and shook if off. Then he punched Damar in the jaw. Damar released his tie and staggered back.

Dub Sac quickly pulled out his 12 gauge and fired one shot to the man's stomach.

Boom!

The impact threw the man against the back wall. He slid down the wall with his eyes open and his intestines hanging out. Damar wiped the blood from his lip, and then ordered the crew to search for Jamerica.

There were three mechanics in the paint bay that heard the gun shot. Two of them were putting a fender on a wrecked Buick and one was prepping an Impala to be sprayed. They all stopped what they were doing just as Taz and Fresh came in with their weapons drawn. They all knew Taz, but didn't know the baldheaded man standing next to him.

One of the mechanics approached them, while wiping grey primer off his hands with a rag. "What's up, Taz? What's the problem?"

Taz lowered his gun because he knew Lando. Lando was brown skinned and stocky. He used to be heavy in the dope game until he caught a sell case five years ago. He did two years in prison for it. During that time he gave his life over to God. All he did now was work and go to church. Taz had no idea he was working here. Fresh, on the other hand, kept his Glock trained on all three mechanics. He didn't know shit about any of them. They all looked grimy to him.

"A girl was kidnapped and we think Gava had something to do with it," Taz said.

While Taz was having a conversation with Lando, Fresh started looking around the shop.

"Naw, ain't none of that going on around here, my brother. God as my witness," Lando said, while placing his right hand over his heart.

"You good, mi breda. I believe you," Taz assured him.

"So what was that noise up front? It sounded like a cannon," Lando said, while glancing over at Fresh.

Fresh was making a lot of noise as he rummaged through their work area. Taz hesitated on answering Lando's question. He knew that if Lando found out that they killed the man up front he might lose his religion today. Hell, for all he knew, the man could be related to Lando. Taz couldn't bring himself to tell him so he just dropped his head.

"What's going on, man?" Lando asked.

Suddenly they heard footsteps coming their way. Taz knew it had to be Damar and the rest of the crew. He had to act fast.

"Listen, mi breda, run while you have a chance."

Lando looked towards the hall and the footsteps were getting closer. He struck out and ran towards the side door. Fresh saw him making a break for it and calmly turned his gun sideways and fired.

Blocka.

The slug took out a big chunk of Lando's chest when it exited. He stopped on his tiptoes and fell on a bag of trash.

After killing Lando, Fresh ran up on the other two mechanics and shot them, too.

Blocka. Blocka.

Then he walked up in Taz's face. His 6'1" frame loomed over Taz as he stared him down.

Damar and the others had just walked in on the stare down.

"What's up, Fresh?" Damar asked, seeing that there was a problem between him and Taz.

"Ya mon, what's up?" Taz also asked, and stepped closer to Fresh to let him know that he wasn't a pussy.

Damar moved in between them. "Whatever beef y'all got, squash it."

"He's the one with the beef," Taz interjected, pointing at Fresh.

Fresh chuckled and tucked his banger.

He then walked by Taz, sucked his teeth. "I got my eyes on you, my nigga"

Then he raised the garage door and went to the van. Damar looked around at the dead men then at Dub Sac.

"Dub, set the place on fire and hurry up. Oga, call Lucky and see where his bitch ass at."

Oga quickly speed dialed Lucky. Lucky picked up on the second ring.

"Yeah mon," he answered.

"Hey breda, we got a problem," Oga said.

Then Damar whispered, "Just ask him where he at."

Oga nodded okay then retracted his sentence.

"Never mind that, but where you at?" After Lucky told him his location, Oga ended the call. "He's in Dade County over his Boopsie's place in Gould's Projects."

"A'ight lets ride. Hey, Dub, hurry the fuck up, my nigga," Damar said, and walked out of the shop.

Chapter 10

An Hour Later

"Ah yeah, suck dat ting, baby. Suck de anaconda real good. Yes whoa," Lucky coached, while caressing the back of Erica's head as she sucked his dick like a popsicle.

She was on her knees and Lucky was sitting back on the couch.

"Umm, umm, you taste good, daddy," Erica said, looking up at him.

"Oh yeah, wait til you taste mi cum. Rude boy been eating fruit all dey," Lucky said, and then chuckled at his comment.

He then leaned forward, licked his finger, and stuck it in her pussy. He twirled it around until it was coated with white cream, and then he sniffed it.

"Umm," he hummed and licked his finger clean.

Boom. Boom. Boom. Boom.

The hard knock sounded like the police so Lucky pushed Erica to the floor, jumped to his feet, and yelled, "Who da bumba clot banging on mi door?"

No one answered but they continued to bang on the door. Lucky found his pants and slipped into them. Then he grabbed his .357 off the coffee table and walked up against the door.

"Who dat?" he asked through the door.

"It's Oga, let me in."

"What up? Why you gotta bang like de damn Babylon?" Lucky asked as he snatched the door open. His hazel eyes widened when he saw Damar and the crew. "Whappen?" he asked nervously.

Damar stepped inside and so did his men. Dub Sac locked the door and pulled out his 12 gauge. Erica came over butt naked and got in Damar's face pointing her finger.

"Don't be running up in my shit like you paying rent. Who the fuck you supposed to be? Where ya badge at, mutha'fucka? Where ya fuckin' badge at?"She repeated the question.

Boo Boo quickly pulled her out of Damar's face.

"Chill, lil' mama, before you get hurt. Our business is with Lucky," Boo Boo said calmly.

"Get your fuckin' hands off me you fat mutha'fucka," Erica screamed as she wiggled from Boo Boo's grasp.

Then she ran and grabbed her cell phone off the table.

"I got something for y'all niggas," she said, and started dialing 911.

Lucky went to reach for her. "No Erica."

He knew she had made the wrong move.

Boom.

Erica's little body flipped over the couch. Dub Sac shot her with the 12 gauge.

"Ahhh, ahhh," Lucky screamed, and aimed his .357 at Dub Sac.

Dub Sac got his shot off first.

Boom.

He hit Lucky in his left shoulder. He fell over on the couch and the shot he let off went into the ceiling. Then he rolled off the couch and tried his luck again. Fresh was quick on the draw and shot him in the chest twice.

Blocka. Blocka.

Lucky dropped his gun and started gasping for air.

"Ahhh, ahhh, ahhh."

His eyes blinked as he ran his hands over his chest wounds.

Fresh saw the frown on Taz's face and didn't like it one bit. He already was suspicious of him due to the incident that happened earlier at the body shop. He didn't hesitate to run up on him, while his barrel was still smoking.

"You got a problem, nigga, 'cause your ass can get it, too," Fresh said, with his Glock glued to his side.

Taz attempted to respond to the threat until Lucky started laughing with blood gurgling in his windpipe.

"Ha, ha, ha, ha, mutha—"

Damar walked over and looked down at him. Fresh and the others came and stood next to him.

"What's so mutha'fuckin' funny?" Damar asked, while mean mugging Lucky.

"Ha, I got your bitch, and your bread," Lucky gargled out, and then he died with his eyes open.

"No, no, don't you die mutha'fucka," Damar screamed and dropped to his knees.

He started shaking Lucky.

"Wake up. Wake up, nigga," Damar continued to yell in deaf ears.

After no response, Damar became desperate and tilted Lucky's head back and started giving him C.P.R. in hopes of reviving him to find out where Jamerica was. While the others stood helplessly, Fresh was cutting his eyes at Taz. His gut feeling was telling him to drop his ass right next to Lucky. After a couple of mouth to mouths, Damar started pumping Lucky's chest.

"C'mon, mutha'fucka, wake yo' bitch ass up. Wake up," Damar cried out.

"Dat nigga dead, bruh," Dub Sac said, while shaking his head.

When Damar finally gave up, he sat up with his back against the couch. His breathing was heavy and he sat there looking into space with blood all over his mouth. His first piece of hope was gone. Fresh stuck his hand out to Damar to lift him up.

"C'mon, cuzo, we gotta keep looking," he said.

Damar took hold of his hand and slowly got up.

"Where we going now?" Boo Boo asked.

Damar sighed and looked at his crew with fire in his eyes.

He wiped the blood off his mouth. "To the warehouse to see if part of what this mutha'fucka said is true."

***

An hour later, Damar found out that Lucky was telling the truth. Five million dollars was gone from the warehouse and so was two hundred kilos of coke. Sad to say, Lucky didn't live long enough to tell him that he took that, too. The only money that the cartel had left was what each of them had on their debit cards.

Damar had stocks and bonds to fall back on until he found another supplier.

By nightfall, Damar was sitting on the dock at his warehouse, putting what he was feeling into the atmosphere. "Damn, baby, I'm sorry. It's all my fault. If you're out there somewhere, you know I won't rest until I find you. If you're in heaven, I pray that you rest in peace and that you and my baby forgive me."

Damar knew she wasn't dead. He still felt her.

Fresh had just got off the phone with Cassie and walked onto the deck to smoke. While lighting his cigarette, he saw Damar sitting at the end of the dock. He inhaled, blew out a cloud of smoke, and then he walked over and sat down beside him.

"You alright, cuzo?" Fresh asked and took another pull of his cigarette.

"I'ma have to be Fresh," Damar said, softly.

"Well, cuzo, if you feel that way, I say we cut the chase and go after Gava straight up."

"I was thinking about that, too, Fresh. It would be like trying to hit a moving target. Plus, we outnumbered like a mutha'fucka. That nigga got an army."

Fresh flicked his cigarette onto the asphalt. "I know your heart is weak right now, but your mind is strong. Cuzo, I wanna tell you something that I never told nobody, not even God. When we was growing up and still til this day, I've always looked up to you. You wanna know why? Because you never gave up and you always knew what to do in any kind of situation, good or bad. I've never seen you afraid of anything—"

Fresh couldn't even finish the sentence.

Today was the first time he ever saw fear in his role model's eyes. Now, he knew how little boys felt when their super heroes were defeated. His eyes glazed over and before he knew it. Three words that he never said to a man before came out of his mouth.

"I love you, cuzo."

Damar slowly turned and looked at Fresh who was looking down at the burning cigarette butt.

Instead of acknowledging what Fresh said, Damar said, "Hey, tell Dub and Boo Boo we 'bout to head out to a hotel. Tell Taz and Oga they can go home now and to get all the money out the streets and holla at me tomorrow. I'll be in the limo waiting on ya."

"A'ight, gotcha," Fresh said.

He stood up and started walking back inside the warehouse.

"Ayo, Fresh," Damar called as he riveted his eyes back to the sky.

Fresh stopped and turned around. "Yeah, what's up, cuz?"

"I love you, too, man."

Frank Gresham

Chapter 11

After leaving the warehouse, Damar thought it would be in their best interest to get a hotel outside of Miami. They drove all the way to Fort Myers and checked into separate rooms. It was a good thing he did because on the way there, Taz called and informed him that the police impounded his van. Apparently, an anonymous person followed and reported the make, model, and color of the van to the authorizes after seeing it flee from Gava's paint and body shop right before it burned to the ground.

***

It was early Monday morning and Damar had just fallen asleep after two days of searching, crying, and praying. He hadn't eaten or washed his ass because he was in that much turmoil. He loved Jamerica just that much, but didn't realize it until the moment she was taken away from him.

Boo Boo went to sleep just before sunrise because he was up half the night arguing with Shonda.

Fresh got a good night's sleep and was up bright and early. He was leaning up against the headboard talking to Cassie, while channel surfing with the remote.

"I'm sorry about your cousin's fiancée," Cassie said softly after Fresh told her about Jamerica being pregnant and kidnapped.

"'Preciate it, baby. I'ma chill here with him for another week or so. At least until he's back to his old self again. You gonna be alright with that?"

"That's fine, Fresh. I truly understand. Plus, your cousin needs you more than I do right now."

"Cool, but enough about that for right now. Tell me how much you miss a nigga and how you gonna fuck the shit out of me when you see me," Fresh said, all suave.

"Whoa, baby, I miss you too damn much. You just don't know, Fresh. When I heard your sexy voice on the phone my pussy damn near jumped out of my panties. She is so wet for you right now. So just imagine what I'm going to do to you when I see you," Cassie said, seductively.

"Damn, guess who just woke up? Ha, ha, ha," Fresh laughed and grabbed his dick.

***

Dub Sac was two rooms down from Fresh lying up with a redbone named China. He met her in the lobby last night on a whim.

China was at the hotel with her boyfriend who didn't know his china doll snorted cocaine on occasions. She snorted the last gram she had yesterday, while her boyfriend was in the shower.

When he finally fell asleep, she decided to sneak out and find herself a quick fix. Fortunately for her, she didn't have to look or go too far. She ran right into Dub Sac at the drink machine. Dub Sac was digging in his pocket to get some change and accidently dropped a gram of coke on the floor.

When China saw the fish scales tumble next to her stilettos, her eyes bucked and she slipped. "Oh shit now."

Dub Sac peeped game quickly and moved in for the kill.

"Dat grown man right there, shawty," he said, and then hit her with his signature laugh. "Hee, hee, hee."

China was wearing the hell out of a black form fitting dress that came up to her juicy thighs. Her stilettos had her standing like a stallion at 5'9". She had jet black hair that came to her shoulders, and her neck, wrist, and fingers were draped in gold. She was ghetto fabulous at its finest.

At first China was reluctant to feed into Dub Sac's tempting statement about his product, but her street instincts told her that he was cool. After looking around to make sure it was safe, she asked him did he have any for sale. *Bam, it was on.* She took the bait. She bought a gram and eased back to her room, but not before asking Dub Sac what room he was in, just in case she wanted more. In less than thirty minutes, she was knocking at his door for some more. She went back and forth throughout the night until she was all out of money. Her last knock of the night was a trick for a treat and she never made it back to her room.

***

Boom. Boom. Boom. Boom.

China and Dub Sac popped up from under the covers when they heard the banging on the door. Dub Sac on impulse reached for his Glock under his pillow. China started feeling around for her panties. She just knew she was busted.

"I hope that aint Driko," she whispered, referring to her huge boyfriend.

Dub Sac frowned and hopped out of the bed butt ass naked.

"Shit, I don't give a fuck. Nigga don't be waking me up 'bout no bitch," he said, and went to the door.

Boom. Boom. Boom.

The knocking continued as Dub Sac looked through the peep hole. Then he looked back at China with a smirk on his face. She didn't see it because she was too busy getting dressed so he decided he would fuck with her dog ass a little bit.

"Hey, shawty, what yo' nigga look like?" Dub Sac asked, looking back in the peep hole.

"He's big and light skinned," she said, hysterically stepping into her heels.

"Yup, that's him knocking. But don't worry, I got something for his monkey ass," Dub Sac said, and spun his gun around his finger like a cowboy.

China held her breath as Dub Sac opened the door.

"Bruh, come downstairs with me for breakfast," Boo Boo said, trying to see the chick standing behind Dub Sac.

"Why you need me to go with you?" Dub Sac asked.

"Nigga, that ain't Driko," China said, peeping around Dub-Sac.

"You know Damar told us not to go anywhere alone," Boo Boo replied, trying to inch his way inside and get a better look at the girl.

"Damn, alright, let me put some clothes on," Dub Sac said, and turned and smiled at China. "Hee, hee, hee, I was just fucking with you, shawty. Dis my nigga Boo Boo. Boo Boo meet China."

China didn't find Dub Sac's little prank amusing at all. She huffed and puffed.

"Fuck you, nigga. I don't see shit funny," she said, and stormed out the room.

"Hee, hee, hee, no, fuck you, hoe. That's why yo' nigga went to sleep on your ass last night," Dub Sac yelled, as she sashayed towards the elevator.

Dub Sac and Boo Boo watched China's ass shake all the way up the hall.

Then Boo Boo looked at Dub Sac. "Ha, ha, nigga, you crazy as hell. Shit, hurry up and put some clothes on. I'm hungry as a mutha'fucka."

"Nigga, hold on and let me hop in the shower right quick," Dub Sac said, heading to the bathroom.

Boo Boo rubbed his big stomach, and then came in the room and closed the door.

"Damn, my nigga, hurry up."

***

Damar was just getting out the shower when his phone started ringing. It was Oga calling.

"Yeah, what's the business?" Damar asked.

"Hey boss, we only collected five hundred grand so far," Oga replied.

"Cool, send half Western Union, and then use the other half for reward money to help find Jamerica. I'm about to email you her picture. I want posters up everywhere by sunset. Hurry up and collect the million you short. I'll make some calls later and try to find some work, but I need that to reup with so get on your job," Damar said, while slipping back into the same dirty clothes.

After ending the call, he concluded that it was definitely time to get some clean clothes. He dialed up the crew and told them that they were about to head out to the mall.

Damar and Fresh went down to eat breakfast and meet up with the rest of the crew. After they finished eating, they all headed out to the mall. They bought some new gear and undergarments. Next on Damar's agenda was to find a house to rent for the time being because it wasn't safe to be riding around in a stretched limo with guns on them. Plus, he refused to stay in a hotel another night.

While Fresh drove up and down the freeway, Damar was on the phone looking for rental listings in the Florida area. Eventually, Damar's time consuming search paid off. He found a cozy brick house with a cobblestone driveway on the country side of Fort Myers in a wooded area. It was the perfect spot for anybody on the run. Damar wasted no time in calling the realtor and dropped seven thousand seven hundred dollars after going to the main office and filling out the proper paperwork under the name Carl Grant.

***

Three Weeks Later

Damar was still running into dead ends, while trying to find Jamerica. He even put up thousands of posters throughout Florida, but he still couldn't get a hit. He hadn't heard anything from Gava, even after he left a trail of dead bodies as he continued to search for his love. He wasn't going to give up hope. He raised the reward money to fifty thousand dollars for any information on his girl. He collected another million dollars from Taz and Oga, which was enough to get back him back in cahoots with Ricardo, who never held a grudge against him for switching to a cheaper connect. Ricardo lived by the old code *money talks, bullshit walks*. He welcomed the King Cartel back with open arms.

Fresh and Boo Boo were finally given a reprieve to go and see their girls, Shonda and Cassie.

Chapter 12

The day after, Fresh finally met Cassie's oversensitive mother and biased father. Then the couple packed and headed to the airport by limo. Five miles up the road, Fresh noticed something was bothering Cassie so he reached over and gently massaged her thigh.

"Hey, baby, you alright?"

Cassie looked at him, placed her hand on his, and sighed.

"I have something to tell you," she said, and dropped her head.

Fresh tightened his lips. "Damn, is it that bad?"

Cassie took a second to think things out in her head before she spoke. *If I tell him, he's sure to drop my ass and that's not what I want. Umm, you know, what if I wait to tell him in front of Damar? That way I can apologize to them both and profess my undying love for Fresh right in front of Damar. Umm, you know, that might make a difference whether he leaves me or not. Yes, yes, that's what I'll do,* she thought to herself.

Cassie held her head up, smiled, and then said, "Hey, baby, it's no biggie. How about I tell you when we get to Miami."

Fresh stared at her real hard. He was trying to read her face, but he saw nothing serious like she said.

"Alright, that's cool," he nodded.

Then Cassie said something to change the vibe going on between them.

"Hey, you know what I've always wanted to do it in a limo," she said, coyly.

Fresh leaned back, grabbed his crotch, and smiled.

"What about dude?" he asked, pointing to the limo driver who he noticed couldn't keep his eyes on the road.

Cassie climbed on top of him, and whispered, "What about him?"

Fresh licked his parched lips, and then put his hand under her dress. He got a hand full of pussy, but not to his surprise. He knew how his girl rocked. The only time she wore panties was when her period was on. He flicked two fingers inside of her in a forward thrust, while pressing his thumb on her clit for extra stimulation.

Cassie moaned as she went in a circular motion.

"Ahhh yeah, whoa ahhh," she cried out.

Fresh grew hard as steel and was ready to get his dick wet. He removed his fingers that were covered with pussy juice and quickly unfastened his pants. Cassie helped him in pulling them down to his ankles. Then she took both hands and began slow stroking him.

"Oh shit, oh," Fresh moaned, and then grabbed the back of her head and guided her down.

Cassie tossed her blonde hair to the side and planted three soft kisses on his apple head.

Muah. Muah. Muah.

Then she went down real slow so she wouldn't choke on the dick. Cassie's head bobbled up and down, and round and round. Fresh was biting on his bottom lip with his hands laced behind his head.

"Ahhh, ahhh, ahhh, damn, baby, that shit feels good," he said, throwing his head back.

When Cassie got his pole nice and wet she sat up, turned around, and straddled him. She then grabbed his dick and stuck it in her pussy.

"Oh, ahhh," she moaned as she gyrated on just the tip of his dick.

Fresh took her by the waist, pulled her down, and added a quick hump.

"Ouch," Cassie yelped and rose up off the dick.

Fresh's pole flopped on his stomach.

"Naw, baby, don't run from the dick. Get back on that shit," Fresh said, pointing to his dick.

"Oh, do I have to?" Cassie playfully asked in a girly voice, while climbing back on top.

Fresh then vice gripped his dick and made it swell up and the veins in it looked like a road map. He then spit on his finger tips and rubbed it on the head.

Cassie braced herself this time with her hands on his knees and slowly came down.

"Ahhh, whoa. Ahhh, yeah. Oh, Fresh," she moaned from the pleasure of pain as she felt his long cock sliding against her tight walls.

After five cowgirl style humps Cassie's snapback pussy was loose again. She then started bouncing on the dick.

Bam. Bam. Bam. Bam. Bam.

Fresh dropped his hands to the side of him and watched with his mouth open as his chocolate pole went in and out of her.

While joy riding, Cassie saw the limo driver watching them through the rearview mirror. Ole dude was all in their video. They say you can sometimes tell what a person is thinking by their eyes and to no avail did the light skin brother's uni-brow deter what Cassie saw in his thirsty eyes, which was good for both of them. Being watched by someone while fucking was another one of the blonde bombshell's moderately fond fantasies. She licked her lips at the driver then she turned her moan up a notch. Next, she held her arms out like she was hula hooping and started moving in a smooth wave like motion.

When the light changed, the driver smirked and gave Cassie a nod of approval for her stellar performance. Then he proceeded on with rush hour traffic.

***

At the same time, Boo Boo was already on the airplane heading back to Miami without Shonda. He decided to surprise her and fly in a day early. Instead of surprising her, his ass got the surprise. He snuck in the house around three in the morning and saw his half brother fucking Shonda from the back.

He was too hurt to confront her, so he just left and headed back to Miami.

Chapter 13

Back in Miami

Boo Boo made it to the house a couple of hours before Fresh and Cassie arrived. He was asleep on the couch when they walked through the door.

"Who is that?" she asked as they tiptoed past Boo Boo snoring like a bear.

"Shhh, that's my nigga Boo Boo," Fresh whispered with his hand on the small of her back.

He led her down the hallway and to his bedroom. When Fresh opened the door and flipped on the lights, Cassie's eyes got as big as quarters.

"Oh my God, it's beautiful," she said, as she tossed her suitcase on the bed.

"Glad you like it, baby, I had someone come in and do it while I was away."

Then she went to touching everything. Fresh knew his girl had an acquired taste. He knew she loved huge beds, and was a plant and animal lover. So he hooked the room up with all her fetishes. He had the king size bed with fluffy pillows on it. He put assorted plants on the window seal and there was wall to wall pictures of exotic animals. Above the headboard was a picture of a white leopard in the snow. Over on the side of the sixty-four inch plasma TV was a portrait of two parrots perched on a mango tree.

Damar happened to be walking by Fresh's room and heard a woman's voice. Then he heard Fresh laughing.

"What the fuck?" he said, and stopped dead in his tracks.

He pressed the side of his head to the door so he could ear hustle. *Damn, I know that voice from somewhere,* he thought to himself. Then he listened a while longer to see if he could put a face to the voice.

"So do you like it, baby?" Fresh asked as he walked up behind Cassie and wrapped his arms around her while she unpacked.

"Yes, Fresh, I love it."

"Ha, ha. That's good, baby," Fresh replied as he nipped at her earlobe.

Damar frowned as he put the name with the voice and a face appeared.

"Oh hell naw," he said, and continued to listen.

Suddenly, Fresh popped the big question.

"So what was it that you had to tell me back in the limo? We here now," Fresh said, and stepped to the side of her to look her in the face.

Cassie sighed and dropped the shirt she had in her hands. Then she turned to Fresh and tightened her lips.

"Fresh, you know I'm madly in love with you, right? I would never do anything to hurt you intentionally. What I'm about to tell you, I should have told you a long time ago."

Damar had heard enough. He was positive it was his Cassie, but he wasn't sure why she came all the way to Miami just to break his cousin's heart. It didn't affect his heart. He really didn't give a fuck about her. But he did care about Fresh's feelings. He was blood so he had to go in and stop her. She wouldn't recognize him with his new face. Damar knocked on the door, and walked in wearing green pajamas with a huge smile on his face.

"What's up, cuzo? I was heading to the kitchen to get something to drink," Damar lied and cleared his throat. "So you must be the one Fresh been beating my ears up about. You right cuz, shawty is fine," Damar said, and gave her a hug.

"Hey, I'm Fresh's cousin Carl," he said, when he broke the embrace.

Cassie turned pale. She was flabbergasted. *So he's staying with two cousins? So where's Damar?* She thought.

She moved her hair away from her eyes. "Yes, I'm his Cassie and it's my pleasure to meet you."

"The feeling is mutual. Hey, you got a good man right here. Better hold on to him, and treat him right," Damar said, pointing at Fresh.

Fresh smiled and nodded. "That's right but she already knows that, don't you, baby?" Fresh asked, looking her in the face.

Cassie put a hand on her hip and finger to her head. "Ummm, I got to think about that one."

"What?" Fresh asked.

Then Cassie slapped her hands on her thighs and smiled. "No, I'm just playing, baby."

Then she stepped to him and put her arms around his neck.

Muah.

"You're the best man a girl could ever have."

Bitch, you on some real bullshit, Damar thought to himself.

"Y'all look good together, cuz," Damar told them.

Then Jamerica popped up in his mind and his pretty smile faded away. *Where are you, my heart?*

"You alright, cuzo?" Fresh asked him.

Damar broke from his trance and exhaled deeply.

"Yeah, yeah, I'm A1 cuz."

"Hey, baby, I'm really tired. I'd like to take a hot shower and go to bed if you don't mind," Cassie said, rubbing Fresh's arm.

"That's cool, baby. It's down the hall, second door to the left," Fresh replied, adding a peck on her nose.

"Thank you, baby," Cassie said, and started going through her bag for her bath accessories.

Fresh walked Damar to the door.

"Hey, cuz, I know seeing me with my girl made you think about Jamerica. I can't imagine how you feel, but life goes on and time ain't gonna wait on none of us, cuz. You got a business to run."

Damar put his hand on Fresh's shoulder and narrowed his eyes. "You right, cuz, and thanks 'cause I needed to hear that."

Fresh smiled. "Anytime, Carl."

Then he shook his head and walked back over to Cassie. Damar closed the door and went back to his bedroom.

Fresh then went and started massaging Cassie's shoulders, "Don't you have something to tell me?" he asked, getting a good whiff of her strawberry shampoo.

Cassie froze because she didn't know what to say now.

"Huh, huh, you didn't tell me we would be staying with two of your cousins."

"Naw, Boo Boo just my homeboy. We all grew up together. Me, him, Damar, and Dub Sac."

"I was referring to your cousin Carl. The one I just met, I thought I was meeting your cousin Damar," Cassie said.

"Ha, ha, check this out. The only reason I'm telling you this is because I trust you."

"Well you did ask me to marry you so you should trust me Fresh," Cassie replied, now facing him with her arms crossed.

"A'ight, a couple of years ago the feds infiltrated us. Somehow they got Damar's girl and blackmailed him. The deal was if he didn't give them a couple million dollars and turn himself in, they were going to stick some major felonies on her." Fresh paused a second to make sure Cassie was following him.

She nodded. "Okay, and?"

"Well, he gave them the money and somehow found a look alike to make the swap."

"Did it work?" Cassie asked in awe.

"Oh, fuck yeah, but Damar was smart. He knew once the feds figured out the man they had in custody wasn't him they would come after him even harder, so he went to Europe."

Cassie shook her head and frowned.

"I'm not understanding," she said, rolling her eyes.

Fresh sighed and touched Cassie's arm. Then he raised his eyebrows.

"He had plastic surgery, baby. Carl is really Damar," he finally said.

Cassie's jaw dropped.

"No, really?" she asked in complete awe.

She was stricken with shock. She didn't know whether this was a good or bad thing. Was Damar mad and just didn't want to show it or did he just not give a fuck?

"Yes, really, but don't repeat this to anybody, especially not him. Remember, you're a stranger to him so he don't trust you. I figured that's why he gave you his fake name."

"I swear I won't tell a soul, baby," Cassie said, softly.

Then she stepped closer to him and looked up at him with her big blue eyes. Fresh leaned forward and kissed her tenderly and gave her a naughty grin.

"I think I need a hot shower, too," he said with a smile.

Frank Gresham

.

Chapter 14

Early the next morning, Damar was sitting up in bed against the headboard on his laptop when an email from Ricardo came in. His first shipment was in Birmingham, Alabama at a warehouse on Black Street. Damar emailed him back to confirm that he would pick it up within twelve hours.

Then he emailed Taz and Oga the directions for the pickup. Next, he checked his email from his stockbroker Tom Prath.

It read: *Hi Carl, Apple's stock fell tremendously the other day. Investors lost nearly $23 billion in stock value. Luckily, I made some trades beforehand.*

"Sorry Tom, I don't need no more buddies. I just need you to keep making me money," Damar said, out loud, and then closed his laptop.

He then hopped out of bed and went to the bathroom. He glanced in the mirror then opened the medicine cabinet, but quickly closed it. He did a double take of himself.

Damn, my nigga, you look rough as a mutha'fucka, he thought to himself. He then leaned closer to the mirror. *Get your shit together, my nigga. She's gone and ya baby is gone. Jamerica wouldn't want you feeling sorry for yourself. She would want you to get on with your life. Plus, there ain't shit you can do to bring them back. You've tried and look at you now.*

"Keep looking," apart of him whispered.

"For what, they're gone," another part of him replied.

Then he dropped his head as he watched the water drip from the faucet. His alter ego spoke to him. *All this sad singing and shit, fuck that! What you need to do is find Gava and cut his fuckin' head off. You ain't never let a mutha'fucka get away with shit so why start now, nigga. King's conquer, and cowards lay down. Which one are you, huh?*

Damar slowly raised his head and peered back in the mirror, but, this time he saw the old gangsta nigga he used to be.

"I am a king, that's what I am."

***

After Damar got dressed, he went and woke up the whole house, starting with Dub Sac.

When Damar knocked on the door, he heard Dub Sac's feet hit the floor.

"It's just me, nigga," Damar yelled through the door.

Dub Sac opened the door and started yawning.

"Ahhh, what's up," he said.

"Shit, 'bout to hit the barbershop. What up, you rolling with me?" Damar asked.

"Hee, hee, hee. Yeah, gimme a minute and I'll be down."

"That's a bet," Damar said, and went and asked Boo Boo.

The trio left in the limo a half hour later heading to *Twin Cutz* on Six Mile Cyprus Rd. On the way there, Damar told Dub Sac that he bet him a haircut that he couldn't answer a riddle that Mario told him a long time ago. Dub Sac figured he could solve a little bullshit ass riddle so he took the bet.

"Okay," Damar said. "If a rooster laid an egg on top of a house which side would the egg roll down?" Dub Sac thought for a few seconds and took a wild guess.

"The right side."

"Nope, wrong answer, my nigga. A rooster can't lay eggs. Ha, ha," Damar laughed. "When we get to the barbershop I'ma tell the barber to hook you up with a nice fade."

"You got me?" Dub Sac asked, and grabbed hold of his hair probably for the last time.

An hour later, they were back on the highway with fresh cuts and shaves.

"Yo, Boo Boo, go by the mall we passed by earlier," Damar instructed once he remembered the road up ahead.

"Cool, you going to meet somebody?" Boo Boo asked.

Damar didn't hear his reply because he had just dialed Jamerica's number for the 50th time. Again, this is what he heard, *the person you are trying to call has a voicemail that hasn't been set up yet. Goodbye.*

Damar signed. He was missing his baby, her sassiness and infectous smile, it all seem like a bad dream but he knew it wasn't. He shook the gloom away then asked Boo Boo "What was that bruh?"

"Who we going to meet?" Boo Boo asked with both hands gripping the steering wheel.

Damar shook his head, and then said, "Naw, we going to buy some tuxedo's for tonight."

"Oh, okay, where we going?" Boo Boo asked, putting his signal on, attempting to switch lanes.

"Miami, big homie. We going to one of the hottest spots downtown, *Club 50.*"

"Hell yeah," Boo Boo said, excited. "I heard about that club and it's supposed to be nice. Tint use to always—"

Boo Boo stopped when he realized he mentioned Tint, their ex-cartel member and childhood friend who ratted on them to the feds.

"Huh, huh, yeah, anyway man I heard a lot of famous people go there. Future, Rick Ross, Chris Brown, 2 Chainz, Lil'Wayne, and Baby. All them niggas, man," Boo Boo said, bouncing in his seat all pumped up.

"Yeah, I heard, but we going on business," Damar said in a relaxed manner. "This morning I came to the realization that I may never find Jamerica. For the last couple of weeks, I've been out of touch with myself. Right now my soul is cold as a mutha'fucka, bruh, and as I think back to all the dirt I've done in my lifetime, I probably deserve to be this way until I'm old. My fear is not death because that's one thing that is promised to all of us. My biggest fear, Boo Boo, is dying in vain. I don't want to go out that way. You feel me?"

Boo Boo felt every word Damar was saying and just nodded while keeping his eyes on the road.

"So in order for that not to happen, I gotta kill Gava. That's the only way I can renew my soul. I want his heart in my mutha'fuckin' hand. You hear me, my nigga?" Damar asked, clenching his teeth and holding his hand like Gava's heart was actually in it.

"Ya, bruh, I hear ya," Boo Boo said, making a right turn at the four way.

"I heard Gava's part owner of Club 50. Seeing him there will probably be slim to none but somebody at that bitch knows where that nigga lay his head. You can bet dat," Damar said, nodding his head very sure of his theory.

"Bruh, please let me kill this pussy when we find him," Boo Boo begged.

"Naw, my nigga, I want him," Damar said, shaking his head.

Then Dub Sac's head popped up out of nowhere with the fresh timp fade, and blurted out, "It's about time for some action. Y'all know killing is my hobby," he sang, while pounding on his chest. "Man, I was getting bored than a mutha'fucka," he added.

Damar spun around with a smirk on his face.

"Damn, nigga, you nosey." Damar shook his head and faced the front. "Dub, you one crazy ass nigga."

"Hee, hee, hee, I know. But I'ma good crazy," he said, and plopped back on the leather seat.

Boo Boo glanced at Dub Sac through the rearview mirror, chuckled, and then replied to Dub's corny statement, "Ain't no such thing as *good crazy*. Crazy is crazy no matter how you put it, nigga."

Dub Sac sat up and looked in the mirror at Boo Boo. "Nigga, you don't know what the hell you talking about."

Damar and Boo Boo then busted out laughing at Dub Sac.

Then Damar cleared his throat. "But at the same time, while we looking for Gava, we gonna ball out and have a good time. Oh, and Taz and Oga should be on their way to Alabama to pick up our first shipment from Ricardo."

"That's what's up. My street soldiers should be about ready to reup," Boo Boo said.

"Cool, you think you can handle Fresh's territories? I'm making him underboss," Damar said, while looking out at the traffic.

"Yeah, I just gotta get with him so he can tell his lieutenants," Boo Boo replied.

Dub Sac then popped his head back up to the front.

"Yo, my nigga, let me take over dem spots."

"Naw, Dub, I'm not gonna fix something that ain't broke. You got the best job in the business."

"Well, right now I feel unemployed," Dub Sac said, jokingly while getting his pack of cigarettes out his pocket. He packed them, ripped the seal off, got a square out, and lit it. "Ahhh," he said as he took a pull.

He blew out a cloud of smoke. Boo Boo reached to his side and hit the switch to crack the window.

"Let me get one," Damar said, reaching over his shoulder.

Dub Sac got Damar a cigarette and handed it to him. Then Dub Sac made a funny jester just to fuck with Damar for his lack of work.

"Hey, man, them shits five dollars a pack. I ain't working right now."

Damar chuckled. "Be patient, my nigga, you might get lucky tonight."

***

An hour later, Damar and his crew were leaving the mall with their black tuxedos for the night. The cool summer day was closing when they arrived at the Holiday Inn near downtown Miami. It was almost sunset. They checked into one suite to be on the safe side since they were back in Miami. Once Damar got settled in the room, he sat at the room desk and opened his laptop. He texted Fresh from a throw-away phone and told him what was going on. Then he called Taz and Oga and told them where to make the drop.

Yo, cuz, we in Miami. I'ma try and find you know who. Damn, I hate to say that mutha'fuckas name, but anyway I need you to hold shit down until I get back. So check this out. Taz and Oga should be pulling up at the house sometime after midnight with a hundred and ten kilos. Put them in the guest house around back. I know we ain't never done this before, but since we on the rebound and Ricardo's coke is so potent, I want you to put a 10 oz. cut on each brick. We'll distribute it when I get back. Oh, and one last thing. I'm moving you up to underboss because I know that you know what to do. I'm trusting you to step up until I get my heard right. Boo Boo gonna be handling your territories so contact your lieutenants and let them know they work for him now. Text me when you handle that."

Fresh replied minutes later, confirming that he received the message.

Chapter 15

Right after Fresh got off the phone with Damar, he had a big smile on his face. He had just finished doing pushups and sit ups. Cassie was lying on her stomach watching TV when Fresh walked by and that's when she saw the smirk.

"Somebody got some good news," she said, propping her hand under her chin, looking curiously at him.

Fresh jumped his sweaty ass on her back.

"Ugh nasty," she said, trying to scoot out from under him.

He held her down and started tickling her.

"I thought you liked when I sweat. You said it turns you on remember."

"But I just got out the shower," she whined.

Fresh rolled over to the side of her. He was damn near out of breath.

"Ahhh, ahhh, ahhh," he panted. "You can take another shower, baby." Then he rolled on his stomach. "Guess what, baby?" he asked with a smile.

"What?" Cassie asked, wiping his sweat off her face.

"Damar just made me underboss."

Cassie raised her eyebrows, and then asked, "And that means what?"

"Shiiit, it means I'm second in command. So everybody except him takes orders from me now," Fresh said, rubbing his chin.

"Aww, that's great, baby," Cassie said, softly and rolled over on her back. "This calls for a celebration," she whispered.

"Umm, umm, you got that right," Fresh said, and slid on top of her. "So where do you want me to take you tomorrow?"

Cassie wrapped her arms around his neck and caressed his baldhead.

"Umm, *Jungle Island*," she said.

"Ha, I knew you were going to say that. Well your wish is my command, baby."

***

Downtown Miami 12 a.m.

Boo Boo parked about a block from the club. There were people lined up from the entrance down to the corner. Damar and his crew were hidden by the limo tint and invisible to the sexy women waiting to get into Club 50. The popular nightclub was known for its rooftop lounge that had a flawless view of Biscayne Bay. The club was also essential for its signature cocktail premier wine list, indoor pool, and popular DJ's.

As Damar puffed on his cigarette, Boo Boo was gawking at the ladies. When the line shortened, Damar spoke with them briefly.

"Tonight we're gonna mix business with pleasure, maybe it will help relieve some stress. So enjoy yourself, but we're still looking for information. Y'all copy?" Damar said, putting out his cigarette in the ashtray.

"Gotcha," Boo Boo nodded.

Then Damar yelled over his shoulder at Dub Sac, "You got that, Dub Sac?"

"Yeah, I got cha," Dub Sac replied.

Damar then loaded his Glock and stuck it under the seat next to Dub Sac's 12 gauge. Next, he looked in the mirror and adjusted his bowtie. Something just didn't look right to Damar so he took it off and unbuttoned the first button on his shirt.

"Yeah, that's much better," he said, then grabbed his Gucci shades off the console and slid them on his face. He then stepped out of the car.

***

When they entered the club, Damar stopped and looked around. Dub Sac was to his right and Boo Boo was posted up on his left. Their matching tuxedos put these boss niggas on display, attracting stares.

No Flex Zone, by Rae Sremmurd was beating hard through the speakers. *No flex zone, they know better, they know better, won a gold medal and a gold bezel, I treat it so special, now ya hoe jealous.*

Boo Boo was bobbing his head, while sweating all the phat asses that passed by. Dub Sac had his poker face on, looking around for the bar.

"You right, Boo Boo, this club be jumping," Damar said as his eyes zigzagged over the clubs stunning interior.

The floor was layered with grained marble and wood. The six-foot Japanese woodblock off to their right was also intriguing to the eye. Straight ahead was the checkered dance floor that was packed like sardines. Everybody was crunk the fuck up. Once Damar spotted the half circle granite bar, he led his crew over to it and they all took a bar stool.

The bartender almost broke her neck trying to get over to Damar and his crew. She knew big tippers when she saw them. She was dark skin with a pretty face. She had on jeans, a white shirt, and a white hat.

"Hey, welcome to Club 50. I'm Sandy. What can I get for you handsome gentlemen tonight?"

Damar placed his elbows on the counter and licked his lips. "Let me have a dirty martini."

Sandy jotted Damar's order down, and then she looked to Dub Sac and Boo Boo.

"And you two," she asked, still smiling, showing off the gap in her teeth.

"Huh, let me get a Hennessey and coke," Boo Boo replied then he turned towards the dance floor and started bouncing on his stool.

"Okay got it, and you, sir?" she asked Dub Sac who was undressing her with his eyes.

"Shiiit, gimme a bottle a Remy and yo' phone number, shawty," Dub Sac said, leaning over the counter and checking out her curves.

Sandy blushed and tried to pull her shirt down over her wide ass, but it didn't cover half of it.

"Okay, one dirty martini, a Hennessy and coke, and a bottle of Remy Martin, correct?"

"Yeah, that's right," Damar nodded.

Sandy then turned around and started making their drinks.

"Hee, hee, hee. You couldn't hide that ass in a U-Haul, baby," Dub Sac said.

Suddenly, Boo Boo spotted a honey on the dance floor dancing with two girlfriends. She was pecan tan and about six feet tall. She was twerking and her booty was rocking everywhere.

"Ayo, Damar, that's my flavor right there," he said, pointing to ole girl.

Damar spun around and pushed his shades up to get a good look.

"Yeah, that's you, my nigga. Shit, go for it," Damar said, before Sandy placed their drinks on the counter.

"Here you go, and that will be two hundred sixty dollars. Can I get you anything else?" she asked politely.

Boo Boo grabbed his drink, thanked her, and broke off to the dance floor.

"Naw, we good. 'Preciate it," Damar said. Then he slipped three hundred dollars from his money clip and handed it to her. "Keep the change, shawty."

"Thank you so much," she said, and stuffed the bills in her apron.

"Hey, what's up with that phone number?" Dub Sac asked then turned the Remy up.

When he lowered the bottle he saw that all three ladies were dancing around Boo Boo.

"Yo, yo, look Damar," Dub Sac said, tapping Damar on the arm.

Damar turned his body halfway around to see what was up.

"Ha, ha, Boo Boo doing the damn thing." Damar said with a smile.

"Shiiit, you good?" Dub Sac asked Damar with his eyes glued to the women grinding up against Boo Boo.

"Yeah, I'm straight," Damar said, and spun his stool back around.

"Cool, I'm finna put some Dub Sac in they life," Dub Sac said, and took off with the bottle in hand. "Yeah, Dub Sac in dis bitch."

Behind his dark shades Damar observed Sandy and the male bartender serving beside her. He was a white guy, maybe in his early twenties. He had brown hair hanging out the back of his white hat and wire frame glasses.

The music was too loud so all he heard was mumbling. He waited another minute before interrupting their conversation.

"Yo, Sandy?" he yelled, motioning for her to come over.

Sandy tossed her rag on the counter and ran over to see what this big tipper wanted.

"Yes, do you need another martini?" she asked politely.

Damar peeped game quickly. Shawty was hoping to get another fat tip. *All bitches love money. I'ma see how desperate she is,* Damar thought.

He leaned over the counter, discreetly pulled out a wad of money, and then asked, "How much for a little information?"

Frank Gresham

Chapter 16

Back at Fort Meyers

Beep. Beep. Beep. Beep.

"That's the truck, baby," Fresh said as he jumped out of bed.

"Umm huh," Cassie said and rolled over on her side.

Fresh slipped on a pair of Michael Kors jeans and a white tank top and went out the door.

Oga was behind the wheel of a burgundy semi when Fresh jumped on the stepladder.

"Yo, pull around back to the guesthouse," Fresh said.

Taz climbed out the passenger side wearing a black Dickie suit and walked to the rear of the trailer. He then guided Oga with a flagger to the front of the guest house.

Once in position Oga got out the cab and went to the back. Taz unlocked the trailer and hit the ramp switch. Fresh walked up the ramp and pulled the blue canvas off the pallets in the rear of the trailer.

"Y'all hurry up and unload this shit," Fresh said.

Oga unfastened the pallet jack and started unloading.

Fresh pulled out his phone to shoot Damar an email. Taz came up beside him. "Where's the boss?"

Fresh was still pissed off about the incident at the service station with Taz. He frowned and looked down at Taz with a gullible smirk and huffed.

"You looking at him. Damar made me underboss."

Taz just stood there. He was trying to think of what to say.

"Ahhh good, I knew it was boun fi. I guess I better get to work, boss," he replied and went inside the house.

"Bitch ass," Fresh said, under his breath.

Oga was coming down the ramp with the first pallet. Fresh quickly cut him off.

"Hey, man, what does *boun fi* mean?"

"It means sure thing to happen," Oga replied and proceeded into the guesthouse.

Fresh sucked his teeth and went back to emailing Damar, letting him know the shipment had made it safely.

***

Back at the club, Boo Boo and Dub Sac had left the dance floor in search of some information.

Damar was still chopping it up with Sandy, the bartender. Unfortunately, even after posing as a music promoter, the only information he obtained was that Gava's business partner was there in his office.

He was a very well known Italian by the name of Sergio Dupree.

After speaking with Damar, Sandy could tell whatever he wanted with Sergio's partner was real serious. She didn't know much about Gava but if he was anything like Sergio, she couldn't imagine what this was about.

Sandy thanked Damar then went two stools down to take an order.

"Hi, I'm Sandy. What can I get you, sir?"

The guy burped and staggered to the counter.

"First, you can give me my damn money back. Whoever made this cocktail needs to go back to bartending school. It tastes like shiiit," the seemingly drunk guy said to Sandy as he waved the empty glass.

He had on a white tuxedo and his red hair was matted on one side from sweating.

"Oh, I'm so sorry. I'll get you another one. What kind was it, sir?"

"Huh, hell I don't know. Just get me another and make it snappy," he said, with a snap of his fingers.

Sandy sighed but started making the drink anyway.

Damar saw that she handled the situation and looked back out on the dance floor. He didn't see his crew but he did spot a fine ass chick looking in his direction. She had on a long silver dress with a pair of four inch heels. Her hair was long and was flowing down her back. Her face favored the actress Lauren London.

The gorgeous woman took her finger and motioned for Damar to come to her. They locked eyes for a moment.

Damar then pointed to himself. "Who me?"

Upon reading his lips she smiled and nodded yes, while swaying her hour glass shape to the beat of, *She Knows,* by Ne-yo. Damar's mind was not on sex, but he went over anyway, maybe he could get some information out of her.

He wiped the corners of his mouth then hopped off the stool and gracefully walked over. First thing he noticed was the rock on her finger.

"Where's your husband?" he asked respectfully.

She shook her head and fingered for him to come closer. Damar shook his head and waved for her to come to him.

She put her hands on her hips and took two sexy strides over.

She met his gaze. "What you scared of?"

When she went to rub his chest, he caught her by the wrist.

"I ain't the one, shawty. Now where yo' man at?"

Little did Damar know, but his mannerism turned her on even more.

She licked her lips. "He's not here."

Then she spun around and wiggled her soft ass against his abdomen.

Shawty a freak, Damar thought to himself as he let her have her way.

When the song ended, she turned to him. "So what's your name, baby?"

"Da, I mean Carl. What's yours?"

"Carl? You don't look like a Carl. You look more like a Damar," she said, and perked her lips out.

Damar frowned. How did she know his name?

"Either you done ran into one of my boys, or your ass psychic. Shit, I hope it's the first one."

"Yup, a little birdie told me," she said.

"Is that right? Well did that little birdie tell you that I don't play no games?"

"Huh," she huffed. "No he didn't have to. I saw that for myself. You see most women have this special ability to sense a man with integrity and you have the look to go with it. That shit is so sexy."

As she went on and on trying to boost his ego, he gave her a pleasant smile. She was telling him some shit he already knew.

"Sooo how about you and I get a room, my treat?" she asked and scratched his stomach with her nails.

Damar gently took hold of her hand and gazed at her wedding ring.

"You never did tell me your name, shawty."

"It's Melissa," she replied modestly.

Damar looked her directly in the eyes, and sincerely said, "Hey, Melissa, check this out. You fine and all and if you wasn't married, I would probably take you up on that. But since you got a man, I can't. I don't know the status on your relationship and I can't give you what you want. But, I can give you some good advice." He then rubbed his thumb over her ring. "Marriage is sacred between a man and a woman. It's being devoted to one another. It's not opening your legs to just anyone who pays you some attention. So if you ain't happy you need to get a divorce. If you are happy, then take yo' hot ass home to your husband, shawty."

Melissa yanked her hand away and drew in a breath. Then she looked him up and down and shot him a bird.

"Fuck you," she said, and stormed off.

Damar smiled. "Well damn."

Then he turned and went back to the bar.

As soon as he sat on the bar stool he saw the drunk guy that was complaining about his drink earlier back at the bar having the same issue as before.

"Listen you baldheaded cunt, why can't you make me a decent drink for crying out loud? I wanna see the fuckin' manager and maybe he can fix me a good drink," he said, pounding on the counter.

Sandy was about to reply until a bartender from the bar on the second level tapped her on the shoulder, and whispered, "Hey, don't give him another drink. It's a scam. He's been getting drinks for free all night."

Now Sandy had a reason to be mad, but still she kept her cool. Here she was trying to please this man and all along he was running game.

"Thank you, Brian," she said to the bartender, and then calmly walked over to the rowdy con artist.

She placed her hands together like she was about to say a prayer.

"Hey, listen buddy, I was just informed not to give you any more drinks. So if you have a problem with that, please take it up with the manager, okay?"

The guy frowned, ran his fingers through his hair and huffed. "You, the manager, and everyone else in this place can suck my cock."

Then he knocked her tip jar over and staggered towards the bathroom.

Damar watched the man walk into the bathroom. He then leaned over the counter and saw Sandy was in a squatting position picking her tip money off the floor.

"You good, shawty?" Damar asked her.

"Not really. He just fucked my night up," she said, not looking up. "I'm sick of this shit. If I didn't have bills to pay I would quit right now," Sandy added, and then stood up with her tip jar. "Where did he go?" she asked out loud.

Damar was nowhere in sight.

Chapter 17

"Ahhh, ahhh, ahhh. You gonna break it, ahhh," the drunk man screamed as Damar had his arm twisted up to his back.

"Shut the fuck up," Damar said, and then drug him over to the stall and started ramming his head into it.

Bang. Bang. Bang. Bang.

After making the man eat steel, Damar grabbed him by the belt loop and stuck his head in the toilet. He held him down for twenty seconds and snatched him back up.

"Ahhh, ahhh, ahhh," the man said, gasping for air.

Then Damar pulled him out the stall and grabbed him by his collar.

"Man, whatever I did to you, I swear I'm sorry," the man pleaded.

"Didn't I tell you to shut the fuck up?" Damar said, and pimp slapped him to the ground. Then he stood over him. "Now get butt naked, bitch."

***

Sandy was wiping the countertop when Dub Sac and Boo Boo walked up.

"Hey, Miss Lady, you okay?" Boo Boo asked, seeing the dismay on her face.

She looked up at Boo Boo, and smiled, "Yes, I'm good, thanks for asking."

"What's up with that number, shawty?" Dub Sac asked.

Sandy shook her head at Dub Sac's determination. He wasn't her type, but she didn't want to dis him in front of his homeboy.

"What kind of girl do you like?" Sandy asked.

"Wet and wild," Dub Sac replied.

"Well I'm not your type, I'm boring. But my girl Jazzy, you'll love her," Sandy said, with a smile.

"Okay, hook that shit up then, shawty," Dub Sac said.

After Sandy gave Dub Sac the girl's number, Boo Boo gave her a gleeful look. "I'm boring, too."

Sandy thought it was cute so she leaned over and pinched his cheek.

"Awe, you look like a big teddy bear."

Then she looked towards the bathroom and gasped for air. Dub Sac and Boo Boo turned around and saw Damar and a naked guy walking beside him.

"What the fuck?" Boo Boo said.

When they reached the bar, Damar shoved him against it.

"What's up, man?" Dub Sac asked, getting in the man's face.

"This mutha'fucka wanted to show his ass earlier so I'm making sure he does it the right way."

"Now apologize, mutha'fucka," Damar seethed between his teeth and gave the man a swift kidney shot.

"Ooh," the man moaned and grabbed his side.

Then he looked up at Sandy. He was dripping wet from the toilet. His red hair was flat on his head and his skin was pale.

"I'm sorry," he said with his teeth chatting together.

Sandy covered her mouth trying hard not to laugh.

"Okay, apology accepted," she said, and whispered to Damar. "Thank you."

Damar winked at her then told the man to get lost.

***

As the guy staggered towards the restroom, Damar looked at Sandy, and then they both broke out laughing.

"I ain't never seen a dick that small before and he told me to suck it," Sandy laughed, smacking her hand on her thigh.

"Ha, ha, ha. That's probably why he's mad at the world," Damar said.

"Whoa, I needed that. I haven't laughed that hard in a long time," Sandy said.

"Hey what's your name, anyway?" Sandy asked, wiping the tears away.

"Carl, and these are my business partners, Boo Boo and Dub Sac."

"Dub Sac? That's a weird name. What's it mean?" Sandy asked curiously.

Damar smiled. "I'ma let Dub Sac tell ya."

At that moment two shadows appeared.

Boo Boo and Dub Sac instantly jumped off their stools and closed the gap between them and Damar.

"What's up? Y'all gotta problem?" Boo Boo asked the two gentlemen standing behind Damar.

"Yeah, 'cause we can fix that shit real quick," Dub Sac added, holding the neck of his bottle.

Damar stood and stepped in between Dub Sac and Boo Boo.

Standing in front of them were two guys, one was a black guy about 6'3", two hundred fifty pounds, and he had a wide nose. He was wearing a black Armani suit with wing tip shoes. The other was a Chinese guy. He was short and stocky with beady eyes and tight skin. He was wearing a blue Armani suit and what looked like slippers on his feet.

"What's up?" Damar asked.

"Mr. Dupree would like to see you in his office about some business," the Chinese guy responded.

"What kind of business?" Damar asked.

"He looking for extra security."

"Cool, lead the way," Damar said, and gave his crew a head nod.

Damar and his crew followed the escorts across the crowded dance floor, through the kitchen area, and into a small warehouse. The black guy knocked on a blue door.

"Come in," someone yelled from behind the door.

The Chinese guy opened the door for Damar and his crew. They calmly walked inside, and stopped in the middle of the floor.

Blam.

The Chinese guy slammed the door behind them, stood guard, and placed his hands behind his back.

Sergio Dupree was sitting behind his cherry oak desk holding up an Esquire magazine. The only thing you could see was the top of his straw Fedora hat.

The black guy whose name was Alto stepped to Sergio's desk.

"Hey, boss, he's here."

Sergio closed the magazine and set it to the side. His skin looked almost orange, and that was probably from a lack of sun block. He had a grey goatee that was trimmed to perfection under his pointy nose. He was sporting a teal blue shirt. You could tell he was a real Floridian. He stared at Damar, while running his hand down his goatee.

"You know, I would have never known who you were until you handled our little altercation at the bar. Quite impressive," Sergio said, pointing to the surveillance monitor on his desk.

"I didn't know we knew each other. I'm a businessman and your boy said you wanted to holla at me about some business. So what's up? You on my time," Damar said.

"Ha, ha, ha," Sergio laughed.

He then opened a briefcase, took out a photo, and tossed it on the desk. Damar looked at Boo Boo and Dub Sac before stepping up to the desk. He picked up the photo. It was a picture of Jamerica sitting in his lap the day she disappeared. An instant sign of grief, anger, and pain seized at Damar's heart.

"Who the fuck took this?"Damar asked.

Dub Sac and Boo Boo then walked up and glanced at the photo.

"Man, what the hell is going on?" Dub Sac asked and braced himself.

Boo Boo turned and did the same. Alto walked up on Boo Boo and cracked his knuckles and growled.

Grrrr.

His tart breath made Boo Boo's nose twitch.

"Chill out, Alto," Sergio said, and sat back and laced his fingers together. "My informant spoke very highly of you. He said you were an intelligent man and I have no doubt that you are. I'm sure we could have done great business together. That is if we would have met under different circumstances. You see, Gava's married to my sister so that kills that idea."

"Okay, if you know who I am, then you know why I'm here," Damar said, walking towards Sergio.

Alto seized Damar's elbow.

Damar cut his eyes up at the muscle man. "Nigga, I will whoop yo' ass."

"At ease, Alto," Sergio said.

The big brute released Damar's arm and stepped back to let him pass.

"Where's my girlfriend and who took that picture, mutha'fucka, since you know so much?"

Sergio smiled, showing his coffee and cigar stained teeth.

"Wait, my informant should be able to answer one of your questions," Sergio said, and pressed a button under his desk.

Beep.

Seconds later, a knock came at the door.

"Get the door, Chun," Sergio said, to the Chinese man.

Frank Gresham

Chapter 18

"Yo, yo, yo, what's up, money?" Mark asked, and promenaded over to Sergio with a lot of hand motion.

"Mark? Man, I thought you was dead?"

The traitor was his IBM tech.

"I knew that mutha'fucka was acting strange that day. I knew it," Dub Sac yelled, while pointing his finger at Mark.

"Ahhh, shut up. Your dumb ass didn't know shit," Mark said, and then sat on Sergio's desk and smiled in Damar's face.

"So you helped them take my girl away?" Damar asked as his right eye began to twitch.

"Call it what you want, money. Only business, man, don't take it personal," Mark said as he picked up the photo of Damar and Jamerica. "Man, great snap shot. Maybe I should be a photographer. Ha, ha, ha."

Damar was steaming now and he knew Sergio wasn't going to let them walk out alive. Neither was he going to die without taking somebody with him. So he bust his move and grabbed Mark by the hair.

With the quickness, he took the palm of his hand and rammed Mark's nose up into his skull. He killed him instantly, Mark hit the floor.

Sergio went for his gun in the desk, but Damar jumped over the table and started punching him in the face before he could grab it. His powerful punches were sounding off like gun shots.

Clack. Clack. Clack. Clack.

Boo Boo turned towards Alto. Alto threw the first blow and caught Boo Boo in the side of the neck.

Boo Boo stepped back and regained his composure. Then he threw a one two jab at Alto and flattened his nose. Alto staggered against the wall. Boo Boo then charged him and they fell on the floor. They began punching each other in the face and in the rib cage. On the other side of the room, Dub Sac was throwing wild blows at Chun. Chun was on his tiptoes bobbing and weaving away from everything Dub Sac dished out.

Out of frustration Dub Sac screamed, "Be still, mutha'fucka."

"Hieeeya, wahh, wahh, yah," Chun said, as he did a round house kick.

He landed the kick and Dub Sac fell into the file cabinet. Dub Sac slowly got back to his feet and wobbled towards Chun with his fist up.

"C'mon, bitch, that's all you got," Dub Sac said. Suddenly, he was hit with two lightning fast knuckle punches to the sternum. "Ughh," Dub Sac hurled over and fell to the floor holding his midsection.

Across the room, Boo Boo had rolled on top of Alto and managed to break free from his grasp. He got to his feet.

Chun ran over and did a flying blade kick to the back of Boo Boo's head and sent him plunging to the floor.

Damar looked up after beating the shit out of Sergio and saw Dub Sac and Boo Boo down. He started looking around the room for something to pick up. He spotted a bag of golf clubs on the far end of the room propped up in the corner.

Chun and Alto came rushing towards him. Damar quickly grabbed everything he possible could off the desk and threw it at them. Then he did a half cartwheel over the desk and grabbed one of the golf clubs.

"What's up now, mutha'fuckas?" Damar asked as he started swinging the club.

Swish. Swish. Swish. Swish.

Alto weaved in and out as he swiped at Damar with his huge hands. Chun tapped him on the shoulder. Alto stopped in his tracks breathing heavy. Chun stepped in front of Alto and stood in place and did a series of jujitsu moves.

"Woo ahh yah, waah yah, aha wooooo," he yelled.

"Shit," Damar said, sensing that his black ass was in trouble.

With agility Chun leaped into the air, it looked like he had strings attached to his back he went so high.

"Hieeeyah," he yelled as he performed his move.

Damar dove out the way and Chun's foot kicked threw the sheet rock. Alto then reached for Damar. Damar side stepped and hit him in the stomach with the club. Alto hurled over then Damar hit him across the back. Alto dropped to one knee.

Chun pulled his leg out the wall and saw Damar attempting to strike Alto again. He ran and did a flip and kicked Damar in the head knocking him unconscious. With Damar down Chun went over to help Alto to his feet. He didn't notice Dub Sac creeping up behind him with a golf club.

Sergio had just come to and saw Dub Sac with the club. Even though he had just taken one of the worse beatings in his life, he mustered up enough strength to retrieve his .38 special from his desk draw.

"I wouldn't do that if I were you," he uttered to Dub Sac.

"Damn, man," Dub Sac said and dropped the club.

Chun then walked over to him and punched him in the stomach.

"Ughh, you mutha'fucka," Dub Sac said as he bent over.

Then Chun chopped him behind the neck. Dub Sac fell flat on his face. Sergio got to his feet. He took his handkerchief and wiped his face.

Alto came over and started dusting the dirt off Sergio's back.

"Fuck this shirt you idiot. Tie them up and take them to Gableton Estates. Bury them on Lot 3 in the cul-de-sac, there's a backhoe on site," Sergio said.

"What about the white boy?" Chun asked, pointing at Mark.

"Take him, too," Sergio said, and grabbed his Faberge cane out of the corner and walked around and stood over Damar. "Cover them up real good."

"Yes, Mr. Dupree," Chun said, and then he and Alto started tying Damar and his crew up.

Chapter 19

It was 2 a.m. and Club 50 was still in full swing. Sandy and Jazzy were out on the loading dock taking a smoke break. It was also a good pastime for Sandy hearing about Jazzy's escapades. Jazzy was the opposite of Sandy all around the board. Sandy was celibate and single. Jazzy was a loose redbone. She wore skimpy clothes and her hair was always done in flirty curls. She was very outspoken and rumors were that her pussy was so good that nigga's made reservations for it. One would think how in the hell did these two become besties. For one, Jazzy loved to tell sex stories and Sandy loved to hear them, since she wasn't fucking anybody and they lived in the same apartment complex building right across the hall from each other.

"Whoa, girl, let me tell you, I met this tall brown skinned nigga last night. He kinda looks like Boris, huh? What's his face, ahhh. Shit, you know who I'm talking about," Jazzy said, as she patted her knee trying to remember the actors name.

"Boris Kodjoe," Sandy said, dryly.

"Yeah, yeah, that's him. Anyway, girl, he said he was going to take me around the world. Honey, I don't think he knew it, but he did that and then some. I think we even fucked on the ceiling, girl. Ha, ha," Jazzy cackled. "Girl, he laid that pipe."

"The ceiling, huh? How did y'all manage to do that? Were y'all on PCP?" Sandy jokingly asked.

Jazzy smiled and pointed to herself, "Pleeeze, leave the jokes up to me."

"Awww, you know that shit was funny," Sandy said, grabbing Jazzy by the jaws and making her lips poke out.

"No, stop, stop," Jazzy said, as she started play fighting with Sandy.

Suddenly, a blue van backed up to the dock two bays down from where they were standing. Chun hopped out of the van and went around the back and opened the door. Alto drug Boo Boo onto the dock. Then Chun went over and helped him tote Boo Boo into the van.

"Look, Sandy, looks like another one of Mr. Dupree's deals gone bad," Jazzy said, nudging Sandy.

"Shit, let's get the hell out of here," Sandy said, and went to stand up.

Jazzy pulled her back down real quick.

"Girl, sit yo' ass down. They don't see us. I heard about Sergio taking people off and killing them, but I never believed it until now."

"Damn, Jazzy, don't you have enough excitement in your life?" Sandy asked between her teeth.

When the girls looked up, Alto was carrying Dub Sac over his shoulder into the van. A few seconds later he came out and went back inside the building.

"C'mon, let's go," Sandy whispered, and she tried to get up again.

"Shhh," Jazzy said, as she pulled Sandy down again.

Alto came back out on the dock this time dragging two men by the collar. A white man and a black one.

"Oh shit, that's Carl," Sandy said, covering her mouth.

"Carl? Who the fuck is Carl?" Jazzy asked, frowning up as Sandy quickly covered Jazzy's mouth.

A second later, Sergio stepped out from the shadows onto the dock with a cigar in hand. He clipped the end of it, and then lit it.

He looked around to see if they were being watched as he puffed away. He just missed Jazzy and Sandy by a couple of seconds. They hid behind the dumpster on the dock.

"Hey, Chun, don't you guys be assing around. Just dump 'em and come back."

***

Gableton Estates 3 a.m.

As soon as Chun passed through the stone entrance of the two hundred acre subdivision, which was under construction, it began to rain.

"Fuck, shit," Chun said, and turned on the windshield wipers and pulled into Lot 3.

He drove around to the backyard. Alto chuckled at how Chun put the two curse words together.

"Ha, ha, ha," Alto laughed because he thought it was funny as shit.

Chun didn't find it funny at all. Plus, he didn't feel like digging a grave at 3 a.m. in the pouring rain.

"You laugh, at me?" Chun asked and put the van in park.

Then he twisted his body towards Alto. Alto heard the seriousness in Chun's voice and looked at his face. It was hard and expressionless so Alto put on his mug.

They stared at each other for a good five seconds before Alto said, "This ain't the time to be getting all emotional, Chun, man, damn. Now c'mon, we got work to do."

He hopped out the van into the pouring rain.

Alto was tough but he wasn't crazy. He knew the *Alto shuffle* that he learned in prison was no match for Chun's fierce jujitsu.

When Alto opened the back of the van, Damar and his crew were sitting up with their hands tied behind their backs. Alto got Mark's body out first and drug it to the designated spot. He then walked back to the van and pulled out his 45 magnum and aimed it at Damar and his crew.

"Hey y'all niggas c'mon out slowly. Move now and don't try nothing stupid," Alto commanded.

Damar came out first, and then came Dub Sac. Chun had just come to the back with a yellow rain coat on. Boo Boo was having a hard time sliding out over the bumper.

"Ha, ha, fat boy," Chun teased Boo Boo as he walked over and sat next to Damar on the wet grass. Damar was in deep thought.

Damn, we always said we would die together, but I didn't think we would go like this. God, if you can hear me, I need you right now. Please help a brother out. Suddenly, he was struck over the head with a pistol.

Clump.

Everything went black and Damar collapsed to the ground. Boo Boo glanced over and saw a trickle of blood going down the side of Damar's head. It hurt seeing his leader like that so he closed his eyes.

As the cold rain came down, Dub Sac rocked back and forth, mentally preparing himself for death.

Chun strutted over and hopped on a backhoe. When he turned the ignition, the monster machine roared like a lion.

RRarrr.

The backhoe crawled forward and the hinged pole on the boom drew backwards to the machine. Then it extended out and the bucket began digging up the first layer of earth.

Dub Sac contemplated on his last minutes alive as the dirt mound grew before his eyes.

Boo Boo was still sitting in silence.

When the hole was about six feet deep and seven feet wide Chun cut the backhoe off and jumped down. He rolled Mark in the hole and did the same to Damar then he stepped back.

Alto moved behind Dub Sac and put his gun behind his head.

"Nigga, you got two ways you can get in the hole, you choose."

Dub Sac huffed, slowly got to his feet, and walked to the edge of the pit. Chun kicked him in the back and he fell into the hole on top of Mark.

Chun pulled his Glock from his waist and pressed it behind Boo Boo's head.

"Your turn, fat boy," Chun said.

Boo Boo didn't budge so Chun raised his arm and slapped him upside the head.

"Ahhh," Boo Boo moaned and fell over on his side.

Chun then shoved him in the hole with his foot.

Thump.

Boo Boo landed next to Damar face down in the mud.

"Oh shit," he cried.

"You a'ight, Boo Boo?" Dub Sac asked as he tried to break the plastic ties on his wrist.

"Ahhh, ahhh, I think my arm is broke," Boo Boo groaned.

Alto and Chun stood over the hole.

"Grab the sulfur and lime out the van," Alto told his partner.

Chun nodded, and then pulled his hood over his head and walked towards the van.

Alto waited impatiently, while the thunder and lightning clashed in the sky.

"Hurry the fuck up," Alto yelled over his shoulder.

Right when Alto was about to go and see what was taking Chun so long, he saw him come from behind the van dragging the bag of sulfur. It looked like he was having trouble with the forty pound bag. Alto met him halfway and snatched the bag up then walked over to the hole.

"Ole weak ass china man," he said under his breath.

He tore the bag open and poured the sulfur in the hole. When the bag was empty, he stood up straight and stretched his back.

"Ahhh," Alto said out loud.

Pow.Pow.

The gunshot echoed through the nearby woods.

Alto dropped the bag and looked down at his stomach. He rubbed his hand over the exit wound, and then gargled up some blood. He slowly fell like a tree.

The gun shot woke Damar and he sat up against the dirt. Dub Sac and Boo Boo looked up and saw the yellow rain coat. Then a bowie knife was tossed down.

Damar shifted to the left and seized the knife. He cut the bonds off his wrist, and then quickly went over to cut Boo Boo and Dub Sac loose.

"C'mon, Dub Sac, lets lift Boo Boo up," Damar said, as he got to his feet.

Boo Boo stood between Damar and Dub Sac. They made a foot sling with their hands and hoisted him up. Boo Boo climbed out the hole. He then pulled Damar up and then Dub Sac. They all stood side by side staring at Chun not sure what was going on.

"So what now?" Damar yelled over the thunder.

The person they thought was Chun removed the hood.

Damar sighed and dropped his head.

God, you something else man, he said to himself. Then he walked over and wrapped his arms around Sandy.

After a moment, Sandy broke the embrace and handed Damar Chun's gun. As she was trembling, she sobbed, "I didn't mean to shoot him."

"Where's that Chinese mutha'fucka?" Dub Sac asked.

Sandy turned and pointed to the van.

"I hit him over the head with a shovel," she said.

"Boo Boo, dump them in the hole," Damar said.

"A'ight, bruh," Boo Boo replied, and then rushed to the back of the van.

"How did you know?" Damar asked.

"Me and my girl Jazzy was behind the club and saw them put y'all in the van. I felt I had to do something, especially after you helped me," Sandy said.

"That's what's up, shawty, and I 'preciate it from right here," Damar said, placing his hand over his heart.

Sandy smiled. "You're welcome."

Damar then stepped to her and put her hood back on her head.

"Where your ride at?" he asked.

"Around front, but it's just a two seater," she replied.

"A'ight, go get in your car before you catch a cold. Just hold tight and don't dip. I don't know where we at so I'ma follow you in the van back to the club."

Sandy nodded and rushed back to her blue Miata.

Boo Boo had just dumped Alto and Chun in the hole when Damar walked up. Damar stood over the hole and shot them both.

Blocka. Blocka.

Dub Sac ran and hopped on the backhoe.

"Now, I'm finna plant y'all mutha'fuckas," Dub Sac said, as he turned on the ignition and went to squinting his eyes down at the gauges and gears. He pulled a lever and the backhoe shifted up. "Whoooo, okay I got it," he said to himself.

Damar and Boo Boo stepped over to the van. Dub Sac looked like he didn't know what the hell he was doing. He pulled another lever and the bucket spun to the left and the bucket crashed into the house.

Ka Boom!

"Damn," Dub Sac said, and quickly shifted the gear down and the boom spun towards the van.

"Oh shit, get down," Damar yelled, and pulled Boo Boo to the ground with him.

The bucket went over the van and made a three hundred sixty degree spin and crashed into a pine tree.

"Hee, hee, hee, my fault," Dub Sac said, and quickly got his ass off the machine before he killed somebody.

Damar and Boo Boo slowly got to their feet.

"Nigga, the way you hopped on that machine, I thought you knew what the fuck you was doing," Boo Boo said, all buck eyed.

"Mannn, I'm just a lil rusty that's all." Dub Sac tried to justify his actions.

Damar was already in the van and blowing the horn at his crew.

"C'mon, Dub Sac," Boo Boo said, and they ran over and got in.

Damar pulled around front and let his window down. Sandy let her window down.

"Yeah?" she yelled.

"Take me back to the club," Damar replied.

"Okay," Sandy yelled, and then she pulled out the driveway and headed back to the club.

Chapter 20

Sandy pulled into an employee parking space at 5 a.m. with Damar right on her bumper. He sped past her car and parked a couple cars down.

"Yo, Boo Boo, how much cash you got on you?" Damar asked.

"I don't know, let me see," Boo Boo said, and leaned over and dug into his pocket.

He pulled out a roll of money.

"Give it to me," Damar said, and Boo Boo handed him the dough.

"What about you, Dub Sac?"

"Hold on," Dub Sac said, and dug into his pocket.

He pulled out two small bankrolls.

"Aight, give me one," Damar said, and Dub Sac tossed him one of the rolls.

"Be right back," Damar said, and hopped out of the van.

He smoothly walked over to Sandy's car. The passenger's side window was already down so he tossed the money in her lap.

"This all I got right now," he told her.

Then he went in his coat pocket, pulled out one of his business cards, and handed it to her.

"Yo, shawty, I wanna thank you again for saving my life. This my business card. Call me if you ever in a jam, a'ight?"

"I will," Sandy said.

Then she wrote something down on a piece of paper.

"Can you give this to Boo Boo?"

Damar took the number. "I got'cha, shawty."

Then he strolled back to the van.

***

Sergio was pacing back and forth in his office trying to call Alto. The phone kept ringing and going to voicemail.

"Dammit," he said, and grabbed his umbrella from the coat rack.

At that moment, Damar and his crew came through the door. Boo Boo had the security guard that was standing outside Sergio's office in a chokehold. When he snapped his neck, Sergio reached inside his coat and grabbed his gun. Boo Boo rushed him and shot him an elbow to the face. Sergio's gun hit the floor and slid under his desk. Boo Boo then snatched him up by his collar. Sergio punched him in the stomach and Boo Boo chuckled and backhanded him.

Clap.

Sergio's arms dropped to his side.

Dub Sac went and retrieved the gun from under the desk. Dub Sac held it up and observed the handgun.

"I'ma add this to my collection," he said, and stuffed it in his waist.

"Throw that mutha'fucka on the desk," Damar scowled.

Boo Boo held Sergio with one arm as he cleared the desktop, and then slammed him on it.

"Ugh," Sergio said.

As Boo Boo held him down, Damar stood over him.

"Dub Sac, take his shoes off," Damar ordered and picked up a golf club off the floor.

Dub Sac slipped Sergio's leather slides off his feet.

"Hee, hee, hee. This little piggy went to the market. This little pig should've stayed his ass home," Dub Sac taunted as he peeled his socks off and dropped them.

"Hey, hey, what are you doing?" Sergio asked petrified.

He was trying to keep his eyes on Damar and wondering what was he going to do with the golf club.

Damar hauled off and smashed Sergio's left foot.

Crack.

"Ahhh, oooh shiiit," Sergio yelled and tried to escape Boo Boo's grasp.

Damar reached down and got one of Sergio's socks and stuffed it in his mouth.

Damar then swung the club overhand and busted his other foot. *Crack.*

Sergio groaned in agony.

"Where the fuck is my girl?" Damar asked.

Sergio mumbled through the sock. Damar snatched it out of his mouth.

"What mutha'fucka?"

Sergio moved his head side to side. "I swear I don't know. I swear."

Damar then punched him in the face.

"You got a picture of me and my shawty so how the fuck you don't know shit?"

"Gava didn't tell me what he did with the girl and I didn't ask. He just told me if I saw you to get rid of you," Sergio sobbed.

Damar then got in Sergio face. "Where's Gava?"

"I don't know. He has houses everywhere," Sergio confessed. "Ahhh, ohhh."

Damar sighed, and stood up and ran his hand down his face.

Then he asked, "Where's your surveillance tapes to the club?"

"Ahhh, over there." Sergio pointed to a door.

"Dub Sac, check it out," Damar said.

Dub Sac quickly went to the room and confiscated the tapes. When he got back, he stood next to Damar.

"Got 'em."

Damar directed his attention back to Mr. Dupree. "Call him."

Sergio slowly slid his hand into his coat pocket and pulled out his cell phone. He speed dialed Gava, but he didn't answer.

"He's not picking up," Sergio cried.

"Try again," Damar ordered.

"Yo, Damar, it's almost sunrise and I think the club 'bout to close," Boo Boo said, looking at the clock on the wall.

Damar grabbed Sergio's phone and stuck it in his pocket.

"Guess I'ma have to work with this. We got all we gonna get out of him."

Dub Sac came over and squeezed Sergio's jaws. He shoved his own gun in his mouth and pulled the trigger.

Pow!

Brain matter and blood scattered on the desk. Dub Sac then stuck the gun back in his waist. Everybody then went for the door. "Hold up," Damar said, glancing around the room. "There's gotta be another exit in this bitch."

He opened a door that looked like a closet, but it was a getaway shaft.

"C'mon y'all," Damar said, and his crew followed him down the slim corridor.

They came out to the back of the club where they were abducted hours ago.

"Alright this the move. I'ma hop in the limo. Boo Boo you follow us in Sergio's van. We gonna dump that piece of shit in the ocean. Then we heading back to Fort Myers."

Chapter 21

Damar and his crew made it back to his house at 10 a.m. It had been a long and unforgettable night. Later that day, the smell of hickory bacon woke Damar. He rolled over and looked at his watch,

"Damn, it's 2 o'clock," Damar said to himself and got out of bed.

He went into his bathroom and hopped in the shower. When the hot steamy water finally relaxed his muscles he stepped out. He heard footsteps in his room and he quickly grabbed his robe and to see who was creeping around in his bedroom.

Cassie was sitting a breakfast tray on his bed. Damar came up behind her quietly. "'Preciate it."

Then he tied his robe. Cassie spun around twiddling her fingers with her head down. Then she looked up at Damar with an intent gaze.

"You're welcome, Damar," she uttered softly. "I cooked enough for everyone."

Damar's eyes widened. *Damn, she knows it's me,* he thought to himself.

"Did Fresh tell you?" he asked.

Cassie paused for a second, and answered, "Yes, the night we arrived. He told me right after he introduced us," Cassie confessed.

"Shiiit, so he knows we use to fuck around?"

Cassie shook her head, "No, he doesn't."

Damar lowered his brow. "So what the fuck you up to?"

"Nothing, what do you mean?"

"Bitch, you knew Fresh was my cousin, but you still fucked him."

"Yeah, you're right, but I never told you I was perfect. I also didn't know I was going to fall in love."

"You full of shit. If you loved him yo' dirty ass would've told him before you came down here."

Cassie lowered her head in shame.

"You're absolutely right. I'll tell him when he gets back."

"Naw, shawty, it's too late. If he finds out now, he's gonna be mad at me and not you."

"It's all about you, huh? Fuck the world."

"In this case, you damn right, 'cause you ain't shit but a piece of pussy."

"You son of a bitch. I hate you," Cassie seethed.

Damar calmly said, "It's mutual."

"Well when Fresh gets here, I'm going to tell him anyway and if he leaves me, I guess we were never meant to be together."

Damar's nostrils flared. He grabbed her by the face and gave her a kiss of death.

Umm, Muah.

When he relinquished, she caught her breath and exhaled. Then she wiped her mouth.

"That's the kiss of death. If you open your mouth, you're a dead bitch."

Suddenly they heard the limo pull into the driveway. Cassie tensed up and Damar looked towards the door. Cassie scurried back to the kitchen. Minutes later, when Fresh came into the house, a hot breakfast plate was on the table. He rubbed his hands together and gave Cassie a kiss.

Muah.

"Ummm, breakfast in the afternoon, thank you, baby."

"You're welcome. Hope you don't mind, but I fixed everybody a plate," she said.

Fresh had just bit into a piece of bacon. He stopped chewing and looked up at her.

"You did?" he asked, not looking pleased at all.

"Oh, you do mind?" Cassie asked.

Dub Sac came in the kitchen when Fresh was about to answer that question.

"Huh, huh, we'll talk about it later," Fresh said, and continued eating.

"Hey, what up, Fresh?" Boo Boo said, and sat his plate in the sink.

Dub Sac also set his plate in the sink.

"Shiiit chillin'. Yo, since y'all finished eating, I need y'all to get that box of cut out the trunk and take it in the guesthouse. It's a hundred and ten keys out there. Damar wants us to put ten ounces of cut on each brick."

"That's bet," Dab Sac said and went out the door.

Boo Boo stepped to Fresh before going out the door.

"Yo, Fresh, you holla at ya folks?" Boo Boo asked.

"Yeah, everything's all set. Taz and Oga should be here about seven o'clock with the rig and your rental car. You'll be following their truck. You got nine counties in Georgia. Drop ten keys in each county. I'm guesstimating after we cut it we should have fifty extra keys. All that's going to Birmingham. I'ma email you all the contact info you'll need before you leave."

"Alright, that's cool," Boo Boo said, and dapped Fresh up.

Then he went out the door.

Moments later, Damar entered the kitchen and put his plate in the sink. Then he sat down at the table across from Fresh.

"How we looking?" he asked as he placed Sergio's phone on the table.

"Everything's good, cuzo. Dub Sac and Boo Boo out at the guesthouse now. Taz will be here this evening and by eight they'll be en route to Georgia," Fresh told him.

"That's what's up," Damar said, staring at the phone as if he was waiting on something to jump out of it.

"Yo, cuz, you didn't need the limo today did you?" Fresh asked as he drank the last bit of his apple juice.

"Naw, I'm just going to lie around and chill. Why? What's up?" Damar asked.

"I'ma take Cassie to Jungle Island and check out that V.I.P Safari tour they got," Fresh said.

Cassie faintly smiled and continued twisting her fork around in her scrambled eggs. She was feeling iffy about her conversation with Damar minutes ago. She wanted badly to tell Fresh about the affair, but right now wasn't the time or place. She would tell him when the time was right.

The whole ordeal was killing her inside and she had to get away from Damar. She quickly stood up from the table and excused herself.

"Fresh, I'm going to freshen up," she said, and sped out of the kitchen.

When Cassie was out of sight, Fresh leaned forward to check out the phone.

"New phone?" Fresh asked, raising his eyebrows.

"Naw, last night at the club—"

Damar spent the next fifteen minutes giving Fresh a recount of last night's events. When he finished the story, Fresh stared at the phone like it was a time bomb.

"Yo, cuzo, you try to call Gava?"

"Yeah, I called about an hour ago. No one answered," Damar said.

Fresh then looked at his watch. Time was ticking and he was dreading the drive to Miami in the limo. It was time to get his own whip.

"Yo, cuz, I think I'ma go car shopping one day this week," Fresh said.

Damar glanced over at him and nodded because it was a damn good idea. It was time to park that old limo.

"Yeah, I think I'ma do that, too, Fresh. Get me a fly ride, a big boy bike, a fancy yacht, and another jet. Oh, and a mutha'fuckin' house my nigga, big as Key West," Damar boasted, while counting his future luxuries on his fingers.

"Hell yeah, cuzo, ha ha." Fresh laughed as he reared his chair back on the wooden floor.

Cassie then sashayed in wearing a pink and white mini skirt, a white top, and a pair of white double strap Giuseppe Zanatti heels. "I'm ready," she said, and then treaded out the door and slammed it.

"What the fucks wrong with her?"

"Shit, that's your girl nigga. Ha, ha," Damar laughed.

"Cuz, I'm out. I'ma fuck wit'cha," Fresh said, and bounced.

***

Damar got up and walked around to the guest house to check on his product and see how Dub Sac and Boo Boo were coming along. Once he saw that they had everything under control, he went back into the house. Sergio's phone was flashing on the table.

"Oh shit," Damar said, and rushed to pick it up.

Gava's name flashed on the LCD screen so he answered it.

"What's up, bitch ass nigga?" Damar blew into the phone as he began pacing the floor. Gava recognized the voice and put two and two together.

"I see you don't know when to back off, but its mi fault. I thought you were just a bad mout boottu. Yo, but yo' gnash is like a saber toothed tiger," Gava said.

"Yeah, I'm that nigga. Now where my girl at mutha'fucka?"

"You know mi wife really sad 'bout her breda Sergio," Gava said, ignoring Damar's question.

"Fuck that, 'cause I'ma kill you, too. Where my girl, bitch?"

"Ha, ha, ha, ha," Gava busted out laughing.

He laughed so hard he started coughing, and then he paused and cleared his raspy throat.

"Yo' girl, I throw her in de wata whey dey. Now she in tha pit of a crocodile's belly. Ha, ha, ha," Gava laughed again.

Hearing what Gava did to Jamerica had Damar's hands shaking. His mouth began to tremble as he ran his hand over his hair.

"Listen, you can run and hide like the lil bitch you are. Remember this, we are in the same business, and from this day I am on a mission to take over all that you have. All that you want to have and there will be no place you will not feel my presence. Just when you think I'm finish, I will kill you, nice and slow," Damar seethed.

"Ha, ha. Yo mon, your booguyaga. You hear me name everywhere, but you will neva see me," Gava replied, and ended the call.

Damar held the phone up, not sure if Gava was still on the line. When he saw that he wasn't, he slammed the phone on the floor. Gava was right in some ways. Trying to get at him would be like trying to touch the President of the United States.

Chapter 22

Over the next three months, the cartel's business sky rocketed.

Boo Boo was still holding his territories down in Georgia and Taz and Oga were still running their same routes through Florida and Birmingham. This still wasn't enough. Damar wanted more.

He went to Ricardo for a big favor. He asked him if he could plug him in with another trafficker.

Ricardo had just the man who was into that type of business. A Korean from Buffalo, New York by the name of Deng Poi. Deng was one of Ricardo's old business associates. Deng had a franchise of seafood restaurants. He had two in Palm Springs, California, one in Laredo, Texas, and five in New York. He had a fleet of rigs he used for product distribution and smuggling drugs.

Deng cut Damar a sweet deal. He agreed to smuggle eight thousand keys a month, a thousand in each truck, and charged him five hundred thousand dollars for each drop. That came out to four million dollars a month that Damar was kicking out for trafficking fees. That was chump change compared to what he was making overall.

As Damar's empire grew he started purchasing things to accommodate his lifestyle. He smooth talked the realtors into selling him the house in Fort Myers and turned it into a stash house.

Then he went to Orlando and bought an Italian style mansion on Orla Vista Ave. What caught Damar's eye about the crib was the beautiful landscaping. It was accented with dogwoods, palm trees, rose bushes, and clay statues of Greek gods.

The driveway was long and it ended in an oval shape with a large bird bath in the center. The ten acre estate was surrounded by an eight foot privacy wall. The patio was surrounding a stunning Olympic size pool that sparkled below the Florida sun.

To the side of the mansion was a ten car garage filled with a fleet of the cartel's latest vehicles. Stretch limos, a yellow hummer, a red Lamborghini, an Aston Martin, two black Cadillac Escalades, a purple 1100 Kawasaki, and twin Suzuki's for Dub Sac and Boo Boo.

Damar didn't stop there with his exquisite exterior layout. He had the interior beautifully designed to perfection. The walls were painted sky blue with white base boards that coordinated well with the white marble floors. He had a seven foot fish aquarium mounted in the wall with piranhas in it. His favorite part of the crib was the living room that he had designed in remembrance of Jamerica. He purchased and placed a white grand piano beneath a ten thousand dollar chandelier. Above it on the wall was a huge portrait of Jamerica.

Damar was back to his old self again. He had his domain looking and feeling like a piece of heaven. Dub Sac and Boo Boo were right there with him enjoying these luxuries.

Fresh, on the other hand, bought him and Cassie a mansion in Miami on East 21st Street. He eventually went car shopping and purchased a sleek black on black Maserati and a bike like the rest of the crew. Shortly after that, he and Cassie went to Key West and had a private wedding. From there they went straight to Puerto Rico for their honeymoon.

Chapter 23

Back in Orlando, Damar had just left his estate on his Kawasaki heading to Daytona Beach for a little R&R and to clear his mind for a couple of hours.

Dub Sac and Boo Boo were waiting on Sandy and Jazzy to arrive at the mansion. The four had been talking on the phone to each other for almost two and a half months and this was going to be their first official date. Boo Boo was in the kitchen sitting at the island bar eating cookies and ice cream. He was wearing a tan Stacey Adams short set. Dub Sac had just fallen up in the kitchen and dapped him up hard. He was holding up a cold glass of twenty grand vodka. He was wearing a pale rose colored Kango, a short sleeve button up that was the same color with a white tank top underneath. He also had on white Nautica pants and white sandals. He had a fat ass diamond ring on his pinky finger.

"What up, my nigga?" Dub Sac asked as he struck a pose, looking like a pimp.

Boo Boo chuckled at the way Dub Sac was standing.

"Ha, ha, ha, boy you a fool," Boo Boo told him.

Dub Sac smoothly walked around the counter and hopped on a high chair.

"Man, let me call Jazzy and see where they at."

Jazzy picked up on the third ring. She was just yelling out the window at a guy driving a gold convertible Jaguar.

"Hey boo," she said, trying to sound sexy.

"What's up, shawty? Where y'all at?" Dub Sac asked, taking a sip of his drink.

"I don't know. Where we at Sandy?" Jazzy turned to her girlfriend.

Sandy glanced down at her GPS, while bobbing her head to Chris Brown.

"We're on Interstate 4. We'll be there in twenty minutes," she yelled over the music.

"You heard her boo?" Jazzy asked Dub Sac as she turned and started back waving at niggas on the sidewalk.

"Yeah, yeah, I heard. Well I'ma fuck wit'cha—" Dub Sac started to say.

"Okay bye, boo," Jazzy said, and hung up before Dub Sac could finish talking.

They were about to roll up on a fine looking brother in a pair of black bikini's. His chest and arms were covered with tattoos and he was walking a blue pit. Jazzy just had to holla at him. She pulled up her bikini top and hung halfway out the window and let her 34 DD's flop in the wind.

She yelled out, "Whoa woo."

***

Daytona Beach

Damar had just ridden into Daytona and was at the red light idling his bike when a green and orange Yamaha stopped on the dime next to him. He glanced at the biker and threw his head up. The biker returned the nod and hit the throttle making the rear tires spin.

Runnn. Runnn. Runnn. Runnn.

Damar was never one to back down from a challenge so he crouched down on his bike and made his back tire spin. When the light changed green both bikes took off. The Yamaha popped a wheelie giving Damar a head start and within seconds he was at 80 mph and then at a 120 m.p.h. As his speed increased so did his adrenaline. He felt the hot wind rolling off his leather suit as he flew pass the spectators. The end of the strip was about fifty yards next to the marina so Damar shifted gears and right when he did, the Yamaha flew passed him.

Zoom.

When the Yamaha reached the finish mark the biker killed the engine and put the kick stand down. A small crowd of on lookers started clapping.

Damar broke his bike down and pulled next to the Yamaha. Since the guy beat him fair and square, he was going to congratulate him on an honest win.

He turned his bike off and hopped off. He then unfastened his helmet and placed it on his hip and walked over to the bike.

"Good race," he said, holding his hand out.

The rider on the Yamaha removed their helmet and curly black hair dropped out. It was a girl with hazel green eyes and freckles. She looked Hispanic. Her flawless skin tone was cashew brown. She gave Damar the prettiest smile he'd ever seen before.

"Thank you," she said, and shook his hand.

"Damn, I got beat by a girl," Damar said, slapping his hand on his face.

"Awe, don't feel bad. I beat guys all the time on this baby," she said, rubbing her hand over the gas tank.

Damar was stuck for a second. Shawty was not only fine as hell, but she also had a voice that was sweet and flowed like honey. All her visible attributes had Damar mesmerized. In the back of his mind he was like, *I'd let shawty beat me in anything.*

"So what's your name, shawty?" he asked as his eyes fell on her peach colored lips.

"Sunja," she replied, sweetly.

"Yeah, that name fits you," he said pleasantly before introducing himself. "I'm Carl Grant."

"Carl, okay that's a pretty common name," Sunja stated.

"I know, but I ain't no common brother."

"Well, what makes you so uncommon, Mr. Grant?" Sunja asked, cocking her head to the side.

Her facial expression conveyed interest.

Damar smiled. "A lot of things that I would love to tell you about over dinner."

"Ummm, so you're asking me out on a date?"

"Yeah, something like that," Damar said and smiled.

"I tell you what. Meet me right here tonight at nine," she said. Sunja started her bike and placed her helmet on. "I hope you can limbo," she yelled over the engine and pulled off.

Damar watched as she sped up the strip.

"Scorpion," he said, to himself, referring to the black scorpion stitched on the back of her jacket.

Chapter 24

"Damn, this house is the bomb," Jazzy said as they drove up the driveway to Damar's mansion.

"Yeah, I know right," Sandy replied, glancing over at the gorgeous landscaping.

When they finally parked, Jazzy pulled out her pocket mirror and applied some lipstick and eyeliner.

"*Whoo*, girl you fine as hell," she said, liking what she saw in the mirror.

Sandy smacked her lips at Jazzy's conceited ass. She grabbed her purse and hopped out the car in a pair of Levi jeans, a white spaghetti strap shirt, and some white coach heels with no makeup.

"Don't hate," Jazzy said to herself as she finished putting her makeup on.

Her phone that was stationed on the console rang. She threw her foundation back in her purse and answered the call.

"Hello," she drug the syllable out.

"What up, Jazzy?" the caller asked in monotone.

"Who is this?" she asked, not recognizing the number.

"This Ced."

"Ced?" Jazzy asked, absentmindedly. "Where I know you from?" she questioned.

"Last week hotel in Tampa. The red Ferrari."

"Oooh, that Ced. Hey, boo."

"Yeah what's up, ma?"

"Oh nothing, what you up to?" Jazzy asked.

"Trying to get with you. I'm in Miami. Where you at?"

At a friend's house in Orlando. I'll be back tomorrow though and maybe we can hook up then.

***

Sandy had just entered the house and Boo Boo greeted her with a light peck on the check and a hug.

"Damn baby, you look good," Boo Boo said, looking at Sandy from top to bottom.

Sandy smiled and put her hand over her mouth.

"Don't do that. I love your little gap," he said, pulling her to him and pecking her nose.

"Aww, you're so sweet my big teddy bear," she said, rubbing his big stomach.

"C'mon baby, let me show you around our crib," Boo Boo said and took her by the hand.

As they walked by the grand piano, Dub Sac was coming from the kitchen.

"Hey, Dub Sac," Sandy said, and waved.

"What up? Where ya girl at?" Dub Sac asked and took a sip of his vodka.

"Huh?" Sandy asked, while looking back towards the front door. "I guess she still in the car."

"A'ight shawty," Dub Sac replied, and headed out the front door to see what was up with Jazzy.

Chapter 25

The Florida sun was beaming down hard and had Dub Sac blocking the rays from his eyes as he walked up next to Sandy's car.

Jazzy was cackling about something Ced had said when Dub Sac's shadow loomed over the dashboard. She looked up and saw his twisted face. Dub Sac knew right off bat that she was on the phone with a nigga by her surprised look.

"Hey, cuz, let me call you back later. I gotta go," Jazzy said, and quickly hung up.

Before Dub Sac could ask a question, she hopped out the vehicle and ravished him like she was overwhelmed with joy.

Dub Sac remained straight faced as she planted kisses on his lips. Despite his touch of jealousy, he did reach around to squeeze her ass. She was looking like a player's dessert in a lime green dress that came four inches down from her tear drop booty. Her pedicured feet were in a pair of Marc Fisher heels and her hair like always was styled in flirty curls. She had large gold loop earrings on.

When she got no lip response, she paused. "You must can't kiss."

Dub Sac grinned to hide his zealous emotions. Then he gave her a sloppy kiss.

Jazzy wiped her mouth. "Naw, you can't."

"Hee, hee, hee, but I can fuck though," Dub Sac came back.

"Huh, whatever," Jazzy huffed and countered. "That's what they all say."

Then she sashayed towards the house. Dub Sac turned and watched her ass jiggle like blubber as she climbed the stairs.

"Yeah, we'll see," he said, and followed her into the house.

Jazzy's eyes lit up when she entered the luxurious mansion.

When Dub Sac got on her heels she spun around. "Whose house is this, really?"

"It's all of ours," Dub Sac answered.

"So what artist do you guys promote?" she asked out of curiosity.

"Shiiit, a lot of 'em."

Jazzy then put her hands on her hips and rolled her neck.

"Like who?" she questioned.

Dub Sac shook his head and motioned for her to follow.

"C'mon, let me show you my bedroom. You ask too many damn questions."

As they headed up the staircase Sandy and Boo Boo were coming out of the den all hugged up and giggling. They came to a halt when they saw Dub Sac and Jazzy. They could see that Jazzy wasn't wearing any panties. Boo Boo's eyes were stuck for a mere second. Sandy cleared her throat.

"You lose something?" she asked.

Boo Boo quickly turned away.

"Your girl Jazzy is a—"

"Yeah I know she's a straight hoe." Sandy finished his sentence. "Yup, she gets around, but I'm pretty sure ya boy gonna strap up, right."

"Yo Dub Sac," Boo Boo yelled.

Dub Sac turned and looked down.

"What's up, my nigga?"

He was holding the small of Jazzy's back.

Boo Boo reached in his pocket and pulled out a box of condoms.

"Here you go," Boo Boo said.

Dub Sac sniggered and tugged at his earlobe, then said, "Naw, I'm good."

He turned and continued up the stairs.

Sandy frowned and looked up at Boo Boo.

"What was that all about?" she asked confused.

Boo Boo covered his mouth and chuckled.

"He gonna use the ear wax test," Boo Boo told her.

"What the hell is that?" Sandy asked, lowering her eyebrows now.

"You really want to know?" Boo Boo asked.

"Yeah, what is it?"

"Well," he sighed. "This may sound a little crazy. See the earwax test is when you take your pinky finger and dig out a little earwax. Then right when you're about to hit that ass you stick ya finger in her pussy. If she flinches the bitch got something," Boo Boo explained.

"Got what?" Sandy asked, tilting her head back and her mouth was twisted.

"A disease," Boo Boo stated with a slight smile on his chubby face.

Sandy paused and stared at him like she missed the punch line.

"Are you serious?" she asked.

"As a heart attack," Boo Boo said, bucking his eyes.

"Baby, I hate to tell you but that sounds like some old fashion bullshit," she bluntly replied, while shaking her head.

Then she glanced down at the box in his hand.

"And what are you doing with them?"

"They're for us, what you think I got 'em for?"

"Okay, well give them to me. I'll hold on to them until that special day comes," Sandy said, taking the box out of his hand and dropping them in her purse.

"I was hoping today was the day," Boo Boo said, pulling her to him and giving her a nice tongue kiss to persuade her otherwise.

Mmmuah, ahhh, ahhh.

When he broke the kiss, he asked with assurance this time, "Now do you want to retract that statement?"

He followed his statement up with a smile.

"Ummm, my teddy bears," she crooned and rubbed his tummy. "I'll think about it," she said, and grabbed his hand. "Let's watch a movie."

Boo Boo sighed and shook his head.

"How can y'all women just turn off just like that?"

Sandy smiled. "Bitches can, hoes can't."

Stating the difference between her and Jazzy. Then she yanked his armed and pulled him into the family room.

Back upstairs Dub Sac was laying on his waterbed, while Jazzy checked his room out. The walls were painted black and clothes covered the hard wood floor. When she went to open the closet he jumped out of bed and ran over.

"Hold on shawty," he said, blocking the door.

He didn't want her to see his arsenal of guns.

"My bad," she said, and turned on her heels. "Turn some music on," she added, while walking over to the dresser.

"Toss me the remote. It's somewhere on the bed," Dub Sac said.

Jazzy fumbled around the covers until she found the remote. Then she handed it to him.

Dub Sac surfed his iPod and put on, *I Don't Mind*, by Usher.

Shawty, I don't mind, if you dance on the pole, that don't make you a ho. Shawty, I don't mind, when you work until three, if you're leaving with me. Go make that money, money...

"Oh shit, that's my jam," Jazzy said, and started singing along.

Dub Sac's eyes were fixated on Jazzy's huge titties. He was dying to see the rest of her.

"Hey shawty, dance for a nigga," Dub Sac said, as he sat at the edge of the bed.

Jazzy turned around and started booty shaking, while her ass was giving him a round of applause.

She looked over her shoulders with a devilish look. "Make it rain, daddy."

Dub Sac didn't hesitate to pull out a bankroll. He slowly began peeling tens, twenties, and fifties from the rubber band and tossed them at Jazzy. As she swayed, she slipped out of her dress and heels.

Dub Sac grinned when he saw her shaved pussy and Serena William thighs. Her stomach was flat and her hips were nice and curvy. Her skin tone was even all over. After Dub Sac finished inspecting her body she twirled around and put her arms around his neck. He pulled her closer and began sucking and squeezing her titties.

"Mmmm, shit," Jazzy said, surprised.

Dub Sac couldn't kiss, but he could suck the hell out of some titties. His tongue made her stop dancing and close her eyes. That's when he stuck his finger in his ear and dug out a small piece of wax. Then he discreetly slipped it in her hole. When she didn't flinch he finger fucked her until she was good and wet. Then he stood up and got butt naked.

"Hee, hee, hee, I'm finna tear dis pussy up," he said out loud.

Jazzy's eyes got big when she looked down at Dub Sac's horse dick. She grabbed it and squeezed. It was hard as a jolly rancher and she felt the instant wetness between her legs.

"Damn, you big," she said, as she stroked his uncircumcised penis.

"I know," he boasted, and then lay her on the bed and put her legs in the buck.

He tapped her clit with the head of his dick three times and slid in. He stretched her walls as he entered. He then locked his arms under her armpits and rammed his long pole up in her.

She gasped then exhaled, and yelled, "Oooh shiiit."

Dub Sac was hitting her pussy like it was his first piece of ass. Their skin was smacking and her pussy slurped.

Flacka. Flacka. Flacka.

Jazzy lashed out a series of cusswords.

"Ouch, ouch, oh, oh. Owl oh fuck. Oh shit mutha'fucka. Oh goddamn, son of a bitch."

Dub Sac then went for her neck and started sucking on it like a leech.

After a few minutes of beating her back out, the pain subsided and she was able to enjoy the dick and concentrate on a nut.

"Oh, Dub Sac, oh yeah, ohhh. Baby, oh shiiit. Yeah, fuck dis pussy, ahhh. That's it, baby. Oh yeah, you mutha'fucka. Oooh," Jazzy yelled as her face reddened and a tear escaped the corner of her eye.

After she came all over Dub Sac's dick, he let her legs down and pulled out.

"Ahhh, ahhh, ahhh," he moaned as he shot milky cum on her belly button.

When the last drop dripped on her thigh he got out of bed. His dick jumped as it slowly deflated. Jazzy was breathing heavy and her legs were up with her feet on the bed and her arms stretched out. Creamy white cum was leaking out of her swollen pussy down to her ass crack.

Dub Sac looked down between her legs and grinned.

"On a scale of one to ten, how would you rate Dub Sac?" he asked.

Jazzy grabbed a pillow and threw it at him. "You make me sick."

Chapter 26

Damar arrived home an hour later elated about his engagement with Sunja. She was on his mind all the way home. It was something besides her beauty that attracted him to her. Right now he couldn't put his finger on it, but he knew he would find out in due time.

He found Boo Boo and Sandy lounging on the sofa. Boo Boo was kicked back like a fat Mack with Sandy's head resting on his chest.

"What y'all watching?" he blurted out.

"What up, bruh?" Boo Boo asked as he threw up the peace sign.

"Hey, Carl, we watching, *The Wedding Ringer*," Sandy said.

"That's what's up. Ay, Boo Boo, let me holla at you."

"Hold up, baby," Boo Boo told Sandy and he got up and walked over to Damar.

"Yo what's up, bruh?"

"Check this out, I'm 'bout to make a phone call, and then I'm heading back to Daytona."

"On business?" Boo Boo asked.

Damar cracked a smile. "Yeah, something like that."

Boo Boo glanced back at Sandy for a quick second. She wasn't paying him no mind. She was all into the movie.

Boo Boo then smiled at Damar. "So what's her name?"

"Sunja," Damar said.

At that moment, Dub Sac and Jazzy entered the room. Jazzy switched her hot ass over and sat next to Sandy. Dub Sac strutted over and joined the fellas.

"What's up?" Dub Sac asked and gave Damar some dap.

"Shit, 'bout to head back out in a little bit. Y'all hold shit down while I'm gone," Damar said.

"We got'cha, bruh," Boo Boo said.

"Hey, Carl," Jazzy yelled, waving from across the room.

Damar leaned to the side of Boo Boo and gave Jazzy a head nod, and then asked, "What's up, Jazzy?"

"Alright I'ma fuck wit' y'all later," Damar said, and went upstairs and turned on the shower.

While he let the hot water steam up the bathroom he called Uncle Henry since he didn't get to speak with him at the funeral.

"Hello," he answered.

"What up, unk? This ya nephew."

"Hey, nep, how you doing?" Uncle Henry sounded elated.

"I'm good. How's everybody doing?"

"We doing about the same. You know Junior getting ready to go to middle school this year. Your aunt still spending all her time at the church. Me, I'm still working at the sawmill. Hey, nep, ya mama's funeral was nice."

"I know it was, unk. Hey, you heard from Vida?" Damar asked, changing the subject.

"Yeah, the feds trying to give her a straight twenty, but I found a federal lawyer that would take the case. He guaranteed me he could get her less than ten years. Only problem is that he wants fifty grand up front. I ain't got that kind of money, nep."

"I tell you what unk, I'ma western union you the money. Don't give it to him until he puts it in writing that he can get her time reduced. Give me his name and number just in case he don't do what he's supposed to."

"Okay, let me get the number right quick."

"Alright, I'll hold."

Uncle Henry was back on the line in seconds.

"You there, nep?"

"Yeah, what is it?"

"His name is Thomas Campbell and his number is 215—"

"I got it," Damar said, as he put the info in his phone. "The money will be there in a couple of hours. Has Valerie called?"

"No, she hasn't. Only God knows where she is," Uncle Henry replied.

"Well tell Junior and auntie I said hello," Damar said, a little disturbed that Valerie hadn't called.

"Okay, nep, and you take care."

"You too." Damar ended the call, got undressed, and hopped in the shower.

Frank Gresham

Chapter 27

Athens Regional Medical Center

Le'Andria, Valerie's nurse was sitting at her bedside in a white scrub with little frogs on it reading the daily bread on her kindle like she had been doing for the last couple of months since they met. Even though they had become good friends, Valerie still didn't disclose anything about her family when Le'Andria asked, so she never brought it up again. Days when it was nice out, Le'Andria would wheel Valerie around the hospital and outside for some fresh air.

But not today, because it was one of those rainy days when gloom filled the sick hospital rooms. Valerie's bones ached and she was in a lot of pain. She didn't have to say it because the frown upon her narrow face said it all. The morphine felt like it wasn't working anymore. She was so weak she couldn't even press the button on the pad next to her. She just stared at it.

Valerie was thirty-eight years old, but now she looked like she was eighty. When Le'Andria heard her grunt, she looked up and saw she was hurting so she quickly pressed the alert button.

"It's going to be okay," she assured Valerie as she patted her hand.

Within seconds, two nurses came rushing to Valerie's aid. They checked her vitals then injected more morphine in her IV line.

Valerie's facial expression and heart rate slowly went back to normal as the medicine filtered through her veins. The nurses propped her head and feet up just a little to help her circulation. Once they did all what was necessary, they left the room. Then Le'Andria went back and sat next to her.

"Feel better?" she asked at a whisper.

Valerie barely smiled. "Yes."

Le'Andria smiled. "Do you need me to do anything?"

Valerie nodded yes, but remained silent for a moment. "Can you read me, *Alone,* by Maya Angelo?"

This was one of her favorite poems when she was in college.

"Alright give me a second and let me google it."

Seconds later. "Okay, here we go."

Le'Andria adjusted her laptop in her lap.

Lying thinking last night
How to find my soul a home
Where water is not thirsty...
And bread loaf is not stone...
I came up with one thing
And I don't believe I'm wrong

Le'Andria was an avid reader and she read the poem with compassion. Each sentence had meaning and truth. Maya's writing was elegant and authentic. It would touch even a fools mind. Her words of wisdom channeled through Valerie's feeble mind as she laid there helpless. She thought to herself, *if I could turn back the hands of time, I wouldn't be where I am today.*

The poem also touched Le'Andria's heart as she read on. At one point, she almost stopped reading to cry, but she knew she had to be strong for the both of them. Just as she uttered the last few words of the poem the monitor went off.

Beep.

Le'Andria saw the flat line across the screen. When she looked at Valerie, her eyes were glazed over and her mouth slightly open. The pain Le'Andria was expecting to feel wasn't there. She thought she would lose it if Valerie died in her presence, but instead she was relieved. Maybe because she didn't have to suffer anymore, or maybe because the poem Valerie requested eased her soul and she died in peace. While Le'Andria was contemplating several nurses and a doctor rushed into the room after hearing the patient alert. It was out of their hands because God had taken Valerie home.

Frank Gresham

Chapter 28

At 9 o'clock sharp, Damar parked in his Lamborghini at the designated spot waiting on Sunja.

She pulled up a minute shy in a 2014 Maroon convertible BMW 18.

"Nice ride," she yelled.

Damar gave her a crooked smile. "It's a'ight. So what's up?"

"Follow me," Sunja said, and pulled off.

Damar followed her about a mile down the strip. She whipped her sports car into a parking lot. The valet opened her car door and helped her out. She tipped him and he hopped in her ride and drove off. Damar inched up and a valet opened his door. He stepped out in a pair of acid washed Versace jeans, a beige short sleeve Versace shirt, and beige and white loafers. He was rocking his platinum necklace with the crown medallion, a diamond ring on his index finger, and a platinum watch and bracelet.

He dapped over to the lovely Sunja and gave her a hug. They said hello between the embrace. Then Damar stepped back to look at her.

Sunja was looking like a Caribbean queen in a green two piece bathing suit with a see-through shawl wrapped around her waist and white Louis Vuitton sandals on her feet. Her hair was in a French bun so you could see her pearl earrings.

"Ummm, you look good to me," Damar said, as he twirled her around.

Her stomach was flat and her ass was plump and firm. It wasn't two big or too small and extending from her pear shaped ass was a pair of well defined legs that were toned to perfection. Damar could tell she did some type of exercising. As he over did her body inspection Sunja shook her head at him and smiled.

"C'mon lets hit the beach," she told him.

***

The beach was crowded. There was something going on over every inch of the sand. From volleyball to bonfires, people were walking and dancing up and down the beach. They were social mingling and just hanging around the bar huts getting their drink on.

The atmosphere was pleasant and peaceful. The cool breeze from the oceans current had cooled the sand off. It was the perfect setting for a couple's night out.

"So who taught you how to ride like that?" Damar asked to start up a conversation.

"My dad," Sunja said.

"Oh okay. You didn't get your looks from him did you?"

Sunja giggled. "No, dad said I look just like my mom."

"You never saw you're mama before?"

"No, she died right after having me."

"Damn, sorry to hear that," Damar said, sympathetically.

"It's okay, my dad's been a mother and a father to me."

"He sounds like a good guy. What's your nationality?"

"My dad is black and my mom was Panamanian."

"Well they sho' made a pretty baby."

Sunja giggled again. Damar looked at her sideways. That was the second time she laughed for no reason. He didn't remember saying anything funny.

"Why do you keep laughing? Is there something on my face or something?" he asked swiping at his face.

"There's nothing on your face, but you just sound—" Sunja paused for a second to think of the right word to say without insulting him.

"Country? Is that what you trying to say?" Damar smiled.

"Yes, yes that's it, but it's kinda cute at the same time."

"Ya, so you feeling this Georgia swag?"

"Ummm, maybe," she cooed.

Damar chuckled.

"You in a bike club? I noticed the scorpion on your jacket earlier."

"Yeah we just started it about six months ago. We have about twenty bikers."

Damar nodded. "That's what's up. So what's your organization about? Y'all just joy riding, hustling, what?

"We're definitely not doing anything illegal. My dad would kill me. He's totally against drugs," she said, shaking her head. "We're just young and having fun."

"I feel ya. How old are you?" Damar asked.

"Old enough," she said, giving him a crazy look.

"Ha, my bad. I know you shouldn't ask a woman her age. Well, where you work at? I know it's cool to ask that."

Sunja smiled. "Daddy doesn't want me to work, and right now I'm going to school to be a doctor."

"How you pay your bills then? Oh let me guess, daddy," they said in unison and laughed together.

"And what does he do for a living?"

"He's president of a bank here in Daytona. Enough about me for now so tell me about Mr. Grant."

"What you wanna know, shawty?" Damar asked and bit down on his bottom lip.

"Awe, I'm starting to love your country grammar," Sunja said, looking at his moist lips.

"'Preciate it," Damar said.

"Are you single 'cause I don't do baby mama drama."

"Yup, no old lady and no kids. What about you? As fine as you are I know you got a piece of a man somewhere?"

"No, but I was engaged once. I've never been in love before. The only reason I said yes was so I could get away and live my own life."

"Well, what happened? Why didn't y'all get married?"

"When my dad found out that my fiancé had just got out of prison he threatened to take me out of his will if I didn't break up with hm."

"So you dumped him?"

"No, I didn't. A week later he dumped me. He said he was joining the military and that I would just be in the way."

"Sounds like some bullshit to me. You think ya dad had something to do with it?"

"I try not to think about it and besides I never asked." She shrugged.

All of a sudden, a burst of fireworks illuminated the sky with a rainbow of colors. Sunja's eyes widened and she took Damar by the hand.

"C'mon, the band is about the start."

Front and center stage was the reggae band Gyptian. They were getting ready to sing their song, *Hold yuh.*

Sunja loved reggae and started winding her hips to the instruments crescendo. *Gyal me wann fi hold yuh. Put me arms right around yuh. Gyal you gave me tightest grip. Me eva got inna my life.*

"Hey, show me what you got Carl," Sunja said, as she took her hair down.

Damar raised his hands and began snapping his fingers to the beat.

"Okay, okay, the boy got skills," she nodded.

"Oh, you ain't seen nothing yet," Damar said, and started really breaking it down.

He crouched down like a surfer riding the waves. Sunja raised her arms and spun around. Damar then made like he was giving her a spanking, while barely tapping her ass. They laughed, talked, and danced through the whole concert.

Next they went to a bar hut and had a few drinks. After a couple of margaritas, they got in the limbo line. From there they went and cuddled up at the bonfire and talked until 3 a.m., and the beach was still jumping with partygoers.

Damar was getting restless. He felt himself dozing off.

"Hey, what's the best hotel around here?" he asked.

"We have a lot of nice hotels here, but you can stay with me tonight if you want. You look tired. You gotta sleep on the couch, though."

"That's cool. Hey, you don't stay with your daddy, do ya?"

Sunja cracked a smile. "Hell no. You really gonna go there?"

Damar grinned, "I'm just saying."

Frank Gresham

Chapter 29

Buzzz. Buzz. Buzzz. Buzz. Buzz. Buzzz.

Sunja glanced up at the clock on the wall. It was 8:15 in the morning.

"Who the hell is ringing my doorbell at this time?" she asked and quickly put the pan of cheese toast on the counter.

She went to answer the door wearing a long t-shirt and panties. She looked through the peep hole and sighed.

"What Rico?"

"Open the door and see."

"No," Sunja said.

"Alright, I'll keep ringing the doorbell then."

Buzzz. Buzz. Buzzz.

Sunja unlocked the door and opened it.

"What do you want?"

Rico frowned up.

"What you got going on?" he asked and pushed his way inside. He saw Damar lying on the couch. "Who the fuck is that?"

Sunja jumped in front of him.

"None of your damn business. Now get out."

"Hell naw," Rico said, and shoved her out of the way.

He rushed over and snatched the covers off Damar.

"Whoa," he said, and threw his hands up.

Damar was laying waiting on his ass. The doorbell had woken him up. He'd been listening and playing opossum the whole time. Last night something told him to grab his strap. Regardless if this was an upscale community or not, he knew a nigga would rob your ass anywhere these days.

"Nigga, you blink wrong and I'll bust yo' bitch ass," Damar said, getting to his feet in just his boxers.

Sunja rushed in between them.

"No, no, don't shot, "she pleaded.

"You told me you didn't have a nigga," Damar said, keeping his Glock on the stranger.

"I don't. He's my half-brother. My dad use to be married to his mother."

"What? Yo' dad got him watching you?" Damar lowered his brows.

"Yeah that's right. I don't know you nigga," Rico shouted.

Damar bit down on his lip and put one in the chamber.

"Nigga I'll—" Damar started to say.

"Nooo," Sunja jumped in front of the gun. "Please put it down, please."

Damar lowered his Glock, he exhaled and decided to hear what she had to say.

Sunja faced Rico with pleading eyes. "Please leave, Rico, please."

Rico slowly back stepped to the door. "You got it," he said and left.

When he went out the door, Sunja slammed the door and locked it. When she turned around, Damar was putting his clothes on. She walked over to him.

"I'm sorry. Now you know firsthand one of the reasons I'm single and never been in love. It's because of my father and his babysitters. Now I guess you're gonna run off like every other guy I've liked, huh? Well there's the door. Sunja said, and took off so Damar couldn't see the tears forming in her eyes.

Once Sunja got in the kitchen, her appetite was gone. She sat down at the table and put her head down. She let the tears fall.

Damar stood in the doorway and watched her cry.

"Fuck," he said, and walked over.

He took a seat next to her. He knew he was original. He didn't like being compared to another nigga. Plus, he didn't want to be compared to another nigga.

"I was in love once. We we're engaged and expecting our first child together. I lost them both," Damar said, softly.

Sunja slowly raised her head and wiped her eyes.

"What happened to them?"

Damar lowered his head and placed his elbows on the table.

"Don't know," he said.

"Tell me how does it feel?" Sunja asked.

"How does what feel?"

"Being in love," Sunja said.

Damar almost smiled but didn't.

"I really can't explain it, but you'll know it the moment it hits you."

"Can you teach me how to love?" Sunja asked.

Damar smiled and reached over and held her hand.

"Love can't be taught, shawty. It has to be showed."

Sunja then got up, walked over, and straddled him. She wrapped her arms around his neck, and looked deep into his eyes.

"Show me how to love."

Damar pulled her close. Their lips were almost touching.

"I gotcha, shawty," he whispered, and they engaged in a blissful kiss.

Frank Gresham

Chapter 30

Five Weeks Later

It was now fall and Sunja was staying at Damar's place more than her own. She went to her place twice a week to make it look like she was still occupying the place, in case her father had people watching her. She wasn't going to let him ruin this relationship.

She liked Damar a lot. He was more than just handsome. He was kind, respectful, and he made her happy. He treated her like a woman and not a child like her father did.

For Damar, the feelings were mutual. Sunja made his rich life complete because she was beautiful, down to earth, and smart.

***

On the way home from their honeymoon, Cassie told Fresh about her and Damar because now she hated Damar with a passion. And she wanted to see him and Damar's bond diminished. Fresh was devastated. Boo Boo had bought a house in Winter Park, only minutes away from Damar's place, for him and Sandy. He made her quit her job at the club.

Dub Sac bought him a condo on Haiwasii Road. He still fucked around with Jazzy on occasions. At one point he tried to lock her down. Her hot ass wasn't ready to settle down no matter how good the dick was. Though she did drop by his crib once a week to break him off, which was fine with him. He didn't mind because business had picked up. Damar gave Dub Sac a list with three names on it. They were people that fucked over the cartel in some type of way and needed to be eliminated.

First on Dub Sac's list was Jamerica's friend Tamika. Damar put her at the top of the list. He wasn't a hundred percent sure if she was the rat that started this chain reaction of bad luck, but he didn't have any doubts either. That put her at number one. Second on the list was Chris Brooks a.k.a. Tech. A known drug dealer who lived in Tangelo Park in Orlando. He got his name from shooting up a club back in the day with a Tech 9. How he got his ass on the hit list was a different story.

Tech started out buying ounces of coke from Coco, one of Taz's runners from Ivy Lane. Ivy Lane is the roughest projects in Orange County.

When Tech got his weight up, Taz trusted and respected his hustle enough to front him a couple of birds. Somewhere down the line, greed kicked in and Tech never paid Coco a dime. A month later, around midnight at a McDonald's, Coco and two others ran into Tech and confronted him about the money he owed Taz. As soon as he did, niggas jumped out of vehicles from all angles and gunned Coco and his men down. No witnesses came forward but two of Tech's men confessed to the murders before any heat came back to him. Everybody on the streets knew Tech was responsible.

Third on the list was Mo from Atlanta. The same Mo that used to work for Damar's Brother Mario. He dodged Dub Sac's bullet a couple of years ago at the club, and vanished the same night Big Swoll was killed. A week ago, a reliable source contacted Damar and told him that Mo had resurfaced and was now a pastor at Summer Hill Baptist Church in Monroe, GA. In Damar's eyes, Mo becoming a preacher was irrelevant because he was a traitor. This hit above the rest was personal, but Dub Sac was on his way to take care of Tamika's snitching ass first.

***

Athens, Georgia, Clarke Gardens Apartments

Tamika was sprawled out on her brown couch with her her legs crossed. She was talking on the phone while the TV was watching her. Suddenly, she heard a knock at the door.

"Kino, hold on," she said, and hopped off the couch and went to the door. "Who is it," she yelled.

"A friend of Jamerica's," Dub Sac said, behind the door.

Tamika quickly opened the door.

"Hey, where she at? Is she alright?" she asked assuming something had happened to Jamerica since she hadn't heard from her in four months.

Dub Sac shook his head. "Naw, she ain't alright. Can I come in?"

***

Rico was outside of Sunja's complex in his silver and black Charger. He had just pulled up in time to see her and Damar walk inside.

Shortly after his run-in with Damar five weeks ago, Sunja's father Joe told him to keep a close eye on her place. He was told to call him immediately if her boyfriend showed back up. Rico did exactly that right after he smoked a blunt of loud.

"Hello?" Joe answered.

"Yo, I'm over at Sunja's and that nigga over here, too."

"Are they inside?" Joe asked.

"Hell yeah. Wait, hold on, they coming back out now. What you want me to do?" Rico asked, looking over his dashboard.

Damar was wearing a black suit by Alexander McQueen and Sunja was looking dazzling in a black Valentino dress and a grey fur coat by Donna Salgers.

"When they leave, go inside," Joe said.

"How I'ma get in?"

"There's a spare key under the welcome mat. Call me once you get inside."

"Alright," Rico said, and ended the call.

He watched with envy as Damar opened the passenger side door to his H2 and let Sunja in. Then he walked to the driver's side, got in, and pulled off.

Damar drove her to a nice seafood restaurant on the marina off the shore. While they were waiting for their dinner, Damar noticed Sunja being very observant of her surroundings. She didn't look nervous just uncomfortable.

"What's up, shawty?" Damar asked.

"Nothing, I'm fine," she smiled.

She really wasn't fine. Her last couple of weeks in Orlando with Damar had been fabulous. There was no one to answer to. There was no one to tell her what she can and can't do. Being with Damar was like being in paradise and she was ready to go back. Damar stared into her hazel eyes until she looked away. He could tell something was wrong.

"Look at me," he said, and then reached across the table and touched her hand. "Do you trust me?"

Sunja looked at him, and smiled, "Of course I do. You've made me so happy."

"Then tell me what's on your mind?" he asked passively. "I don't like secrets."

"I'm afraid, Carl. I'm afraid that my dad is going to find out about us and break us up."

"Listen, ain't nobody gonna run me off. I can promise you that," Damar said, with confidence.

Sunja squeezed his hand. "Well I've made my decision and I don't want to stay here anymore. I'm going to rent my condo out."

Damar grinned. "So where you gonna live?"

Sunja tilted her head.

"Oh it's like that?"

"Ha, you know I got you, shawty. We'll slide by your crib after dinner and load what we can in my truck, a'ight?"

"Wise man," Sunja said.

"Yes, I am. I chose you, didn't I," Damar said, and caressed her hand right as the waiter popped up with their food.

Hours later, Joe Richerson was in his den sitting at his desk looking over some bank statements when Rico rang the doorbell. His Spanish maid, Marie, answered the door.

"Hey, Marie," Rico said, and waltzed past her. "Where's Joe?" he asked.

"He's in the den, senor," Marie said, fanning her face because Rico smelled like a pound of weed.

Rico made his way to the den and saw Joe sitting at his desk. Joe was a very classy dresser. Joe wore a caramel brown suit by Emilio Pucci with black loafers that went well with his dark complexion and his salt and pepper hair.

Rico's bright clothes invaded Joe's peripheral.

"Don't you get tired of wearing red?" he asked, not looking up.

"Nah, red is a dominant color," Rico replied.

"Yeah, and so is black," Joe said, and took off his glasses. "You get what I ask for?"

Rico then reached inside his coat and pulled out a zip lock bag containing two glasses that he took from Sunja's place. Joe nodded his approval, then picked up his phone and dialed Glenn Pierce, who was a detective and a good friend of his in Dayton. Glenn recognized the number.

"Hey, Joe, how's it going?"

"I'm making it," Joe said, and then stood to his feet and walked over to the window. "Hey, Glenn, I need a big favor."

"Yeah, what is it?" Glenn asked.

"I need you to check some fingerprints for me. I have them here on a couple of wine glasses," Joe stated.

"Okay, no problem. Meet me at my office in about an hour," Glenn replied.

"Thanks, I'll see you then," Joe said, and hung up.

Frank Gresham

Chapter 31

A Day Later

Fresh finally built up the nerve to confront Damar about Cassie after weeks of holding it in. He woke up hurting all over again, until the bottle of Ciroc kicked in when he was halfway to Damar's place. The more he thought about Damar and Cassie together, the madder he got.

I risk my fuckin' life for this nigga. Whatever he told me to do, I did it, and not once did I complain. This how he do me. Well nigga you gonna have to show me what you know today, Fresh said to himself as he whizzed through traffic, while being the perfect example of a D.U.I. in his Maserati.

***

"Oh Carl. Oh yeah, ohhh," Sunja moaned as she rode Damar on his leather sofa.

They both were tipsy from the bottle of Moet that they emptied, and then threw on the floor along with a bed of red rose petals. Sunja's head was spinning like she'd been on a Ferris wheel, but she still rode the dick like a jockey.

She came up on the tip, and then she constricted her pussy walls.

Damar sucked his teeth. "Ahhh."

Then she came down real slow and gyrated her hips twice, and then came back up again.

"Oh shit," Damar said.

He was shocked at this new trick Sunja pulled out the bag. She had never fucked him like this before. She was in beast mode. Damar could smell her fruity pussy juice in the air. *Damn, I should've made your ass leave Daytona a month ago*, he thought to himself as he buried his head between her perky breasts.

"Oh yeah. Oh Carl, oh," Sunja crooned as she put her arms around his neck and grinded faster.

Her light sweat was warm and Damar could feel her heart beat. He pulled her close and began sucking on her hard nipples.

"Ummm, ummm, ummm," he moaned, while massaging her soft ass.

"Ahhh, ahhh," Sunja moaned as tears of joy cascaded down her cheeks.

Then she stopped and grabbed Damar by his face. They both were breathing heavy. Damar saw the tears and gently wiped them away.

"Why you crying, shawty?" he asked.

Sunja leaned up and kissed him tenderly.

Then she looked into his eyes. "Now I know what love feels like."

Damar licked his lips.

"So do you like it?" he asked.

Sunja sniffled and smiled. "Yes, but do you love me?"

Her voice trembled. Damar grinned and rubbed the side of her face.

"I can't lie shawty, cupid shot me in the ass, too."

Suddenly, the doorbell interrupted their confessions.

"Damn, who the fuck is that?" Damar asked. "Hold up, boo, and let me get that."

Sunja stood and slipped on her robe. Damar put his pajama pants on and walked to the door. He looked threw his peep hole.

"Oh, it's Fresh," he said, and opened the door.

Fresh staggered in with a bottle in his hand.

"Nigga, you drunk?" Damar asked, having never seeing Fresh that way before.

Fresh spun around and laughed. "Ha, ha, ha, nigga. What the fuck it look like?"

Then he gave Damar an evil stare. Damar stepped to him and looked at him as if he was crazy.

"Cuz, what's your problem?"

"Nigga, you my problem," Fresh said, and stepped closer.

Damar glanced over to Sunja.

"Hey, baby, give us a minute."

Sunja rose up.

"Sit," Fresh yelled.

"Sunja go upstairs 'cause this nigga drunk," Damar said.

Fresh snatched his Glock from his waist and pointed it at Sunja.

"Bitch, I said no. Now sit your ass down."

Sunja quickly sat back down on the couch.

Damar frowned. "Cuz, what the fucks wrong with you?"

Fresh then pointed the Glock at Damar and took a deep breath, "Why didn't you tell me about you and Cassie?"

Shit, Damar thought to himself. He started to blow and roast her mutha'fuckin' ass, but he knew that wouldn't be a good idea right now since Fresh had the upper hand. He had to finesse him because he knew he wasn't in his right mind. The last thing he wanted to do was die over a bitch.

"You came over here pissy ass drunk to confront me about a piece of ass? Damn, cuzo, did you have a blood transfusion or something? We kings, nigga, and don't nothing come before family," Damar said.

"I can't tell, nigga. You got me looking like a goddamn fool," Fresh said, waving the gun.

"Chill, cuz, you drunk. Just think about it. She got you looking like a fool. She's the one you need to be checking, not me. Money over bitches, nigga. We was raised off that shit," Damar said, with emphasis.

"Shut up, shut up," Fresh yelled with tears in his eyes.

"I can't, Fresh. I'm the realest nigga I know and you know I'ma tell it like it is. So if you wanna pull the trigger, you gonna have to shoot me in the back," Damar said, and turned around.

"No, turn yo' ass back around. Look at me, nigga. Look at me," Fresh screamed.

Damar figured he would have a slow reaction because he was drunk. So while he was talking he ducked, did a leg sweep, and kicked Fresh's leg out from under him. Fresh fell on his back and the bottle shattered. The gun slipped out of his hand and slid across the floor. Damar then dove on top of him. Fresh had no fight in him. He just closed his eyes real tight. Damar drew back to punch him, but he couldn't bring himself to do it. He knew his cousin just fell in love with the wrong hoe. Shit happens, but at the same time, his thoughtless actions disgusted him to the core. He let him go and walked over and picked his gun up. He discharged the clip and kicked the single slug out the chamber. Then he tossed the gun back to Fresh.

"Get the fuck out my house you pussy whipped ass nigga. I don't want that shit rubbing off on me," Damar said.

Fresh struggled to his feet, cradled his Glock like a baby, and looked at Damar all teary eyed.

"Cuz, I'm sorry, man," he pleaded.

Damar turned his nose up. "Sorry ain't gone get it, I want you to kill that hoe."

Fresh slowly nodded and turned to leave.

Damar grabbed his arm and whispered, "Not that I don't trust you, cuzo, after you kill her bring me her pretty little head."

Then he gave Fresh a pat on the head and calmly walked him to the door. When he turned around, Sunja was still in a state of shock. Damar knew he would have to explain to some degree so he walked over and sat down to console her.

"Sorry about that, shawty. Are you a'ight?" he asked and embraced her.

Sunja closed her eyes and sighed.

Then she looked up. "Should I even ask?"

"Ask, 'cause I ain't got nothing to hide."

Sunja shifted to face him and shot him a grimacing look.

"Who was that and who the *fuck* is Cassie?"

"That was my cousin Fresh and Cassie is his wife."

Sunja frowned, "You fucking her?"

"Naw, baby," Damar shook his head. "We use to fuck around before they hooked up. I guess she finally told him. That shit was a long time ago."

Sunja took a breath. "Please don't be playing with my heart."

Damar smiled and took her hand.

"You ain't gotta worry, baby. You got my heart. It's just me, you, and God, okay?"

"Okay, so does this mean that you're ready to take that picture down?" Sunja asked.

Damar then glanced up at Jamerica's beautiful picture, and then back at Sunja.

"Yeah, I'm ready."

Frank Gresham

Chapter 32

Two Days Later

Sunja was pulling into her condo complex to get the rest of her clothes when all of a sudden a caravan of unmarked cars surrounded her vehicle. She slammed on the brakes and almost got whiplash from the sudden stop.

"Oh shit," she grabbed her neck.

The sunrays coming through her windshield momentarily impaired her vision until her head stopped spinning. Then her door was snatched open and she got out the car slowly.

"Ms. Richerson," someone called out. "Are you alright?"

"Sunja, Sunja," another person called out.

She recognized it to be her father's voice and called out to him. "Daddy?"

"I'm here, baby girl," Joe said, and grabbed her.

Then a horde of federal agents seized her car.

Sunja looked up at him. "Dad, what's going on? What are they looking for?"

"We're going to get to that, but first I wanna make sure you're alright," Joe said, showing more concern about his daughter.

"Oh my neck," she cried.

Joe turned to Glenn Pierce angrily. "She was about to park so you didn't have to do that."

Sunja interjected, "Dad, what's going on?"

Glenn Pierce held his hands up and shook his head.

"Sorry, Joe, it wasn't my call."

Then a huge black guy busted through the chaos wearing a beige suit.

"I made the call," he said, waving his badge. "Detective Fred Brown. Mr. Richerson, shall we step inside?"

"C'mon, baby, let's get this over with," Joe said, ushering his daughter into her condo.

Once inside, Detective Brown pulled out a large envelope and took out some photos. He lined them up on the kitchen counter.

"You see these?" Brown asked.

Sunja carefully looked over the pictures.

"Do you recognize any of these men?" he asked.

"Yes, him and him," she said.

"Names please," Glenn said.

"This one is my friend Carl, and this one is his cousin Fresh. Why?" she asked.

Then Detective Brown pulled two more photos and set them side by side.

"Do you know this guy here on the left?"

Sunja shook her head. "No, can't say that I do."

"Well these two guys are the same person. He had plastic surgery done. His real name is Damar Val King. He's on America's Most Wanted list for conspiracy and murder charges."

Sunja gave the detective a horrid look. "What the fuck are you talking about? You must have the wrong person."

"No, ma'am, fingerprints don't lie."

Sunja then looked over to her father.

"Dad what is he talking about?"

Joe took hold of his daughter and gave her a mournful look.

"I'm sorry, baby. You know how protective I am over you. I had Rico come in here and get a wine glass that had your friend's fingerprints on it. I gave it to Glenn to check them out. Once he found out who they belong to, he contacted the feds."

Then Glenn jumped in again. "They directed me to Detective Brown here."

Detective Brown then interrupted. "He connected to a murder."

"You're lying," Sunja shouted. "Dad, I can't believe you would make up something so cruel just to see me unhappy. How could you?"

"No, Sunja, I swear I'm not making this up." Then he looked at Detective Brown. "Tell her the rest detective."

Detective Brown cleared his throat, and continued, "Damar is the ring leader of The King Cartel. A very dangerous organization. Ms. Richerson this man is a manipulator. He uses people. He's killed many men, women, and even children. I know this is a shock to you, but we need your cooperation to get him off the streets. We take down the head the rest of his empire will fall."

Sunja's heart almost stopped when reality kicked in. Her first real love was with a stranger. She fell into her father's arms and broke down crying. A flood of tears dampened his shirt. Joe propped his chin on her head and his eyes began to water. He knew it had to be love. Sunja never cried this hard for anything or anyone.

He rubbed her head affectionately and looked at Detective Brown with sadness in his eyes. "When are y'all gonna get that son of a bitch?"

"As soon as she tells us where he's at," Brown said.

Sunja slowly raised her head. Her face was pale and her eyes were swollen. Snot was running out her little nose.

"Dad," her voice cracked. "I love him."

Joe pulled her closer. "No, baby, you have to let him go. He's a killer. Help them bring him in, please. When you love someone, you don't lie to them, Sunja."

"Your father is right, Ms. Richerson. Where is he now?" Detective Brown asked.

Sunja wiped her face then looked at Detective Brown. He was mean looking and his facial features were hard. Then she looked at Glenn Pierce. Glenn was a baldheaded light skinned brother. He had a narrow face and a pencil thin mustache. He didn't look as mean.

He looked more trustworthy so she asked him, "Can you promise me you won't hurt him?"

Glenn glanced at Detective Brown who nodded his agreement.

Joe rubbed his daughter's hair. "Do the right thing, baby. He doesn't love you."

Sunja walked over to the kitchen sink and stared out the window. *I knew it was too good to be true. He played me like a fool. He told me everything that I wanted to hear and I fell for his lies and charm. My dad's right, he doesn't love me. It was all a dream,* she thought to herself. Then she walked back over to her father and the detectives. She sighed.

"We were supposed to meet at seven o'clock at the *AMC Downtown Disney Theater*," Sunja admitted, and then she ran into her father's arms.

Detective Fred *Bad Ass* Brown smiled. He didn't do that very often. He then glanced at his timepiece.

"Okay, it's 5:30 right now. We have an hour to get there and thirty minutes to set up the task squad." He then turned and shook Glenn's hand. "I appreciate your services. The feds will take over from here." Then he turned to Sunja. "Ms. Richerson, I need you to wear a red shirt so you'll stand out. I'll fill you in once we get there. In order for this to work, I'ma need you to act normal as you possibly can."

Sunja nodded. "You're not going to shoot him, right?"

"Right. Just don't make him suspicious of anything. Don't do nothing out of the ordinary. Just watch your body language and face expressions. If your emotions kick in, I need you to get up and go to the ladies room. However, for your safety and others, there will be a sniper present. Mr. King is considered armed and dangerous. One false move and he won't hesitate to start shooting," Brown confirmed.

"I understand," Sunja said.

"I'll be close by, baby girl." Her father said, rubbing her shoulders.

Detective Brown jerked his head towards Joe.

"No, Mr. Richardson, that's a conflict of interest you can't be there."

Then he got on his phone and walked out the door in a hurry. Sunja and her father then embraced upon his departure.

Frank Gresham

Chapter 33

AMC Downtown Disney Theater, 7:25 P.M.

Sunja was sitting in her car with the heat on. She was very nervous. Her hands trembled as she put on a light coat of lip gloss. She then glanced in her rearview mirror. Her eyes were red so she put some Visine in them to clear the redness. Suddenly, a burnt orange Aston Martin pulled up beside her.

Beep.Beep.

When the window came down, Damar had a huge smile on his face. Sunja smiled back but her emotions started running wild, and her heart was racing.

Damar stepped out the car wearing a leather jacket, Levis, and a pair of rust color Sperry top shoes. Like a gentleman, he came over and opened her door. Sunja got out wearing a red Alfani sweater, blue jeans, and a pair of black rider boots.

First thing Damar did was kiss her.

Muah.

She was so distraught that her lips didn't respond. Damar lifted her chin.

"You a'ight, shawty? You been talking about Jurassic World all week."

Sunja forced herself to look into his eyes.

"Baby, I'm just cold," she said, and rubbed her hands together.

"Okay, well let's go inside," Damar said, and they walked into the theater, unaware of the sniper on the rooftop and the unmarked cars in the parking lot where Detective Brown was watching from a far. He had five agents inside dressed as civilians and wearing earpieces.

Once Damar and Sunja were inside, Detective Brown turned the dial up on his headset.

"Agent Morrell, I want two men on the back row once they're seated. Then I want two around the concession area. I need you posted near the restrooms. When the movie is over she's going to the bathroom and stall for approximately twenty five minutes. That's enough time for the theater to thin out. When I give the signal, *take him out*. He killed one of ours so this mutha'fucka don't deserve to live."

"Yes, sir, I copy," Agent Morrell said, and gave his men the orders.

While the feds were getting in position, Damar and Sunja were at the concession stand. The theater was nice and warm and very crowded. All you could smell was popcorn.

"Ahhh that smells good, don't it?" Damar asked, looking at the mounds of buttery popcorn in front of him.

Sunja raised her eyebrows. "Ummm, yummy."

"Okay, one large popcorn," Damar told the cashier. Then he turned to Sunja who was looking off in another direction. "Hey, baby, what else you want?"

Her head whipped around and their eyes met. She didn't blink. She froze up like she was taking a picture.

The ten year veteran Agent Morrell read Sunja's face from a distance. She was nervous. Agent Morrell's sixth sense was keen as a K9. He was dark skinned, short, and buff. He had a high fade cut. He moved smoothly through the crowd, while speaking to Detective Brown on his earpiece.

"Sir, Brown, sir."

"Yeah agent what is it?" Brown asked, keeping his eyes on the entrance.

"She looks like she's about to fold. I'm moving in closer," Morrell said.

Fred Brown nodded his head.

"Roger that," he replied.

Damar placed the back of his hand across her forehead and she was warm.

"Damn, baby, you running a fever. C'mon, I'ma take you home," he said.

"Baby, I'm good. Get me some chocolate covered peanuts, please."

"Ha, alright baby." Damar turned to the cashier. "Let me get some of them chocolate peanuts and a large sprite."

***

Halfway through the movie, Damar noticed Sunja was getting fidgety. She kept sneaking glances around the theater. This made him a little paranoid. *Something ain't right,* he thought to himself. Then he glanced around the dim theater.

On the second row, he saw a white guy that looked out of place. He was young, bare faced, with a military cut. What aroused Damar's suspicion about him is he watched him for two minutes and not once did he look up at the screen.

Then Damar looked to his rear and one black dude made eye contact with him. Damar thought he would turn away, but he didn't. It was like he deliberately wanted Damar to know he was watching him.

Damar calmly turned his head to the movie. He cut his eyes at Sunja. The rims of her eyelids were filled with water. She blinked and a huge tear rolled down her cheek. *Damn, shawty done set a nigga up,* Damar thought to himself. He reached in his coat and took the safety off his Glock. He contemplated his next move for a minute.

"You know Sunja, I've always wondered how my life could have turned out if I hadn't lost my father at a young age. Or if I had finished high school and went off to college. I probably could have been President of the United States, who knows."

Sunja looked over like, *Where did this come from?*
Damar continued with pain in his voice.

"That wasn't my destiny. Even though I was dealt a bad hand, I made the best of what I had. When I made it to the top, I blessed a lot of people. I gave to the homeless. I built recreational centers for children. I did all this and more, but nobody gave me a pat on the back for that shit, you feel me? Good news is no news to a lot of people. Do something wrong and the whole world will know. Shits crazy, and that's why I stopped giving a fuck about what a mutha'fucka thinks about me a long time ago. They can't feel my pain. In less than three years, I've lost my brother, my mama, my girlfriend, and my unborn child. I said all this to say, I could have all the money in the world, but it means nothing without love and loyalty. Now I have nothing worth fighting for, but my life because the one I loved and trusted sold me out."

Sunja looked at him and his eyes were sad. Then she flashed back to the kind man she fell in love with. She was no different from those that judged him. The detective had instilled in her mind the same persona they had of him. She was wrong because those were things of his past. She knew God was the real judge and jury not man.

She turned back to the screen and spoke to him indirectly.

"After the movie, I'm supposed to go to the bathroom and they're going to arrest you," she said, barely moving her lips.

Damar's jaws tightened then he looked at her. Her eyes remained glued to the movie.

"Why you telling me now?" Damar asked.

"I don't want you to go to prison. At first I did, but now I don't."

"What made you change your heart?" he asked.

"I love your ass that's why." She broke down and started crying. "I thought we were going to be together forever. You lied to me, you lied."

Damar sighed, "I'm sorry, but I had to. Then he calmly got up and walked to the bathroom.

One of the agents that was sitting on the back row notified Agent Morrell that the suspect was on the move. Agent Morrell was in line at the concession stand when Damar entered the men's room.

"All units stand down. Looks like he just going to use the bathroom," Agent Morrell said.

Damar immediately rushed into a stall and closed the door. He sat on the toilet and contemplated on how he was going to get out of there. *C'mon, nigga think of something,* he thought to himself, while looking around.

Then he heard someone come in the bathroom. He peeped through the door crack and saw two white guys. As he looked them over, he knew they weren't the feds. They looked more like college kids. They were speaking broken English and it sounded like they were from England. After they primped in the mirror one left and the other went into a stall and dropped his pants to take a shit.

Damar crawled in the stall and the man's eyes widened.

"Hey man, what are you doing?" the man asked.

Damar quickly jumped to his feet and put the man in a chokehold. After he passed out, Damar stripped him. He then took off his clothes and put the man's clothes and hat on. He propped the guy in a sitting position on the toilet. *Now I gotta sneak outa here.* Then he heard someone come into the restroom. He looked through the crack in the stall, there was a young black kid standing at the sink. Then an idea came to mind.

Damar walked out the stall and approached the boy, "Aye, kid, do you want to make five hundred dollars?"

The kid looked at Damar in shock and said, "What I gotta do?"

"I need you to go out there and start a fight with somebody." Damar branished his gun and said, "I don't throw away money. So make that shit happen."

The kid left in a hurry and in less than a minute, Damar heard the commotion outside. So he calmly walked out the restroom, he held a vice grip on his Glock underneath the brown blazer. The right coat sleeve was empty. Damar had cuffed it and tucked into the pocket. *C'mon, you almost there,* he said mentally as he headed towards the exit. With beads of sweat trickling down his face and spine, every face he looked into on his way out looked like a police. It felt like all eyes were on him. All it would take is for one mutha'fucka to move wrong and he was going to light this bitch up like a New Year's Eve party.

Once he made it outside the fall breeze cooled his face and sent chills down his damp back. His heart was beating like a Congo drum. *Damn, I'm pretty sure their watching my car*, Damar thought to himself. So he walked up to the sidewalk and flagged a cab down.

Agent Morrell paid for his drink, and then glanced at his watch. Ten minutes had passed. *He should be out of there by now,* he thought to himself as he walked towards the bathroom. He walked inside, flashed his badge to three men, and waved them to step out. He cautiously looked under each stall and saw some clothes on the floor and someone sitting on the toilet. He slipped his gun from his holster and tapped on the door.

"Damar King, this is Agent Dwayne Morrell. We have the place surrounded. Come out with your hands up or on the count of three I'm coming in." Morrell nervously counted to three, and then he kicked the door in.

Boom!

"Shiiit," he said, and snatched his radio from his hip and ran out the bathroom. "All units, the suspect is on the run. I repeat, the suspect is on the run."

In seconds, the theater was surrounded with law enforcement officers. Detective Brown was standing amongst all the commotion shouting and cussing, while his officers combed through the parking lot looking for Damar. Sunja walked through the chaos and went un-noticed to her car. That made it easy for Sunja to sneak out the theater and drive away in her car.

Suddenly, Agent Brown stopped in his tracks, he grabbed his radio. "Agent, Agent," he yelled.

"Yes sir," Agent Morrell said.

"Where's Ms. Richerson? Where the fuck is she?"

Agent Morrell shrewed his shoulders. "We lost her, too, sir."

"Goddammit," Detective Brown said, and slammed his radio on the pavement.

Frank Gresham

Chapter 34

When Damar arrived at his mansion, he called Boo Boo and told him what happened and to handle the business until he got back. He was leaving the state. He then went upstairs to pack. While he was packing his Tom Ford bag, someone walked into the room. He grabbed his Glock off the bed and spun around. It was Sunja.

"How you get in?" he asked.

"My key," she said, and started towards him.

He raised his gun and she stopped.

Then he asked, "Are you alone?"

"Yes, I am," she replied. "I snuck off just like you did. Don't worry, I wasn't followed and they don't know where you live."

Then he barked, "A'ight, so what the fuck you want?"

Sunja got down on her knees. "I want you."

Damar frowned. "I don't fuck with snitches."

Then he tucked his gun, zipped his bag, and walked around her. She grabbed his leg.

"Please take me with you, pleeeeze," she begged.

Damar stopped and looked down at her.

"Why should I?" he asked.

"Because I love you with all my heart. God as my witness, I'm sorry I made a mistake by judging you like everybody else. When you left the theater I pictured I'd never see you again, and my heart almost stopped. That's why you should take me with you."

As Sunja looked up at Damar, tears were streaming down her face and she held on to him a little tighter. Damar relaxed his shoulders and took a minute to absorb what she'd just said. *If the shoe was on the other foot, he thought to himself. I would've been mad too, if she lied to me.*

He wouldn't have done what she did, but he knew women reacted off emotions. The truth hurt her and she acted out of anger. Now there wasn't a doubt in his mind that she did love him.

She was at his feet begging just to be with him, and knowing the consequences would take away her freedom. He glanced up at the ceiling. "A'ight, God, you ain't never steered me wrong."

***

New Jersey

Damar and Sunja arrived at *Liberty International JFK Airport* three hours later. It seemed longer for Sunja because Damar spoke to her in one word sentences. He wasn't angry anymore just nervous. When they got off the Challenger 605 private jet, they caught a cab to Manhattan and checked into the Hilton Hotel with the fake ID Damar had made several weeks ago and got a room on the 14th floor.

First thing Damar did was hit the shower to replenish himself. While he was lathering up, Sunja slipped into the bathroom. He saw her undress through the blurry glass pane as she tiptoed over. She stepped in and walked under the showerhead. Damar searched her hazel eyes for clarity. *Will she be loyal and will she adapt to my world?*

Sunja searched his eyes for forgiveness. *Will he trust me long enough to prove my love for him?*

Though doubtful, their love for one another made their hearts overpower their thoughts. They exploded into an ecstasy of salvation and started ravishing each other with hard kisses. Damar picked Sunja up by the waist and she wrapped her legs around him. He pinned her up against the tile and rammed his dick into her pussy.

"Ahhh, ahhh, ahhh, ahhh, ahhh," she moaned and clawed at his back.

"Who's pussy is this?" he asked.

"Ahhh, ahhh, ahhh. This your pussy, baby," she moaned.

Damar pounded her pussy for twenty minutes nonstop. Then he stepped out the shower and carried her to the bed. The intensity increased when he laid her down and put her legs on his shoulders. Sunja tried to run up the headboard, but Damar held on to her waist as he plunged deep inside of her.

"Oh shit. Oh, oh, oh fuck," she screamed and came all over his dick.

She was so loud Damar was sure they heard her in the next room. Right when he was about to nut, he pulled out and stroked himself. Sunja quickly seized the dick and started smacking the head on her tongue. She moaned with anticipation. She was ready to taste and swallow his cum.

"Ummm, ummm, cum for me, baby," she said, between licks.

Damar felt the tingling sensation.

"Oh fuck," he moaned as thick white cum skeeted in her mouth.

Then she swallowed half of him and started sucking his dick dry.

"Ummm, ummm, ummm," she hummed as salty cum coated her throat.

When she was done, Damar plopped on the bed. Sunja laid on top of him and caressed his chest.

"I love you," she whispered.

Damar rubbed the back of her head affectionately. "I love you too, shawty."

Sunja then asked, "What name do you want me to call you, Carl or Damar?"

Damar grinned. "Whichever one you want, baby."

Sunja started flicking her tongue around his nipples, and then she slid down and licked his navel. She then grabbed his semi hard dick, and started sucking it until it was standing at full attention.

She glanced up at him. "I like Damar better."

***

Morning

Damar woke up drained and hungry. He looked over at Sunja and her pretty little head was nestled on the feather stuffed pillow. The satin sheets stopped at the crack of her ass. He gently pulled the sheet to the middle of her back. Then he leaned over and kissed her face.

"Ummm," she moaned knowing her man's touch.

Damar got out of bed and took a quick shower. He then slipped on a white Gucci sweat suit with the shoes to match and he dabbled on some Gucci Guilty cologne. While he was primping in the bathroom mirror, Sunja came in walking like a duck.

"What's wrong with you?" Damar asked with a smile on his face.

He knew damn well why she was limping. If her pussy was a car it would be in the junkyard right now.

Sunja smiled and stepped in the shower.

"Don't act like you don't know."

"Ha, ha, my bad. Hey, baby, I called room service and breakfast is on the way up."

"Okay," Sunja yelled over the running water. "Baby, after breakfast, can we go to the spa? I desperately need a back rub."

"A'ight, that's what's up," Damar said, and stepped out the bathroom to call Dub Sac.

He walked over to the window overlooking Manhattan. Dub Sac answered on the second ring.

"Yo what up, bruh? Boo Boo told me what happen."

"Yeah, I'm good, though. I'm out of state right now. I need you to watch my crib," Damar said.

"Alright, my nigga, I gotcha. Ayo, I took care of that bitch Tamika, I'll tell you about it when I see you in person."

"Oh, fo'sho," Damar said.

"I'ma get at Tech this weekend. I just found out he be over some broad's house in Richmond Heights. Some bitch named Monica," Dub Sac said.

"A'ight, my nigga. Handle dat and I'ma fuck with you later," Damar said.

"Peace," Dub Sac replied and ended the call.

Then the doorbell rang.

"Room service," someone yelled.

Damar opened the door and was greeted by a waiter. He wheeled the food cart onto the plush carpet. After he placed the silver platters on the elegant tile counter. Damar tipped him real good and he backed the cart out the room with a smile on his face.

When Damar finished setting the table Sunja's sexy ass came over with a blue towel wrapped around her.

"Umm, looks good," she said, pointing to the sliced kiwi.

While Sunja was looking over the rest of the breakfast, Damar was looking over her. Her jet black hair was wet and curly. She looked exotic. Her face was radiant. The hot shower had exfoliated her skin from last night's impurities. She looked so delicious that Damar wanted to throw her ass on the plate.

She looked up and saw him gawking so she made a funny face at him. She crossed her eyes and stuck out her tongue.

Damar laughed. "You still fine."

Frank Gresham

Chapter 35

After breakfast Sunja put on one of Damar's sweat suits because she didn't have a change of clothes. Then they went to the spa located on the third floor. The receptionist was tall and brown skinned with too much makeup on.

"Welcome to the Hilton Spa. Is this your first time here?"

"Yes," Sunja said.

"Do you have a room here at the hotel?" the receptionist asked.

"We have a room," Damar answered.

"Would you like to charge this to your room?"

"Yes please, room 1427," Damar said.

"Okay, what would you like done today."

"We want a full body massage in the same room, please." Sunja said.

"Sure, follow me," the receptionist said.

She took them in a dressing room and gave them directions on what to do. She turned and walked away.

Minutes later, after they changed into their robes, another young lady came in all excited, and said, "Are you ready for your massages?"

They responded, "Yes."

She walked them into the massage room.

There was two petite Asian masseuse's standing by each flatbed. They greeted them and asked them to remove their robes and lay down on their stomachs. Then the Asian women covered their lower half with a sheet and started massaging them.

As Damar and Sunja lay adjacent from each other their minds slowly drifted.

Damn, I wonder if Fresh gonna kill that hoe Cassie. 'Cause I hate to have to kill my own flesh and blood. But I will, because I have a business to run, with or without him, Damar thought to himself.

Umm, this feels good. Oh, I gotta go shopping. I don't have any clothes. Then I wanna go to The Lion King Theater. I heard the play is breathtaking. Tonight I want to go to a real nice Italian restaurant with my man. Damn, I love him, Sunja thought with a happy smile drawn on her face.

Then Sunja opened her eyes and saw Damar gazing at her. She smiled and made a funny face. Damar chuckled, and then made one of his own. He drew his lips back, bared his teeth, and crossed his eyes up. He looked like Jamie Foxx when he played Wanda.

They both busted out laughing.

Suddenly, Damar's phone rang. He reached over and picked it up. The caller ID read, *Restricted.* He didn't answer it. They called right back and this time he took the call.

"Yeah, who is this?" he asked.

A voice came through the phone.

Damar's heart started beating so hard, it felt like it was coming out of his chest. He quickly sat up on the flatbed, his voice trembled, "Jamerica, is dis you?"

A desolate cry came over the phone, "OMG, Damar, yes, baby It's me."

To Be Continued...
The King Cartel 3
Coming Soon

Coming Soon From Lock Down Publications

LOVE KNOWS NO BOUNDARIES **III**

By **Coffee**

THE KING CARTEL **III**

By **Frank Gresham**

BLOOD OF A BOSS **III**

By **Askari**

BOSS'N UP **III**

By **Royal Nicole**

A DANGEROUS LOVE **VII**

By **J Peach**

GANGSTER CITY

By **Teddy Duke**

SILVER PLATTER HOE **II**

By **Reds Johnson**

BURY ME A G **III**

By **Tranay Adams**

THESE NIGGAS AIN'T LOYAL **III**

BY **Nikki Tee**

DON'T FU#K WITH MY HEART **III**

By **Linnea**

BROOKLYN ON LOCK

By **Sonovia Alexander**

THE ULTIMATE BETRAYAL II

By **Phoenix**

THE STREETS BLEED MURDER 2

Frank Gresham

By **Jerry Jackson**

<u>Available Now</u>

LOVE KNOWS NO BOUNDARIES **I & II**
By **Coffee**
SLEEPING IN HEAVEN, WAKING IN HELL **I, II & III**
By **Forever Redd**
THE DEVIL WEARS TIMBS **I, II & III**
and BURY ME A G **1 & II**
By **Tranay Adams**
DON'T FU#K WITH MY HEART **I & II**
By **Linnea**
BOSS'N UP **I & II**
By **Royal Nicole**
A DANGEROUS LOVE **I, II, III, IV, V & VI**
By **J Peach**
CUM FOR ME
An **LDP Erotica Collaboration**
THE KING CARTEL
By **Frank Gresham**
STREET JUSTICE **I & II**
By **Chance**
THESE NIGGAS AIN'T LOYAL **I & II**
BY **Nikki Tee**
A HUSTLA'Z AMBITION **I & II**
By **Damion King**

SILVER PLATTER HOE

By **Reds Johnson**

LOYALTY IS BLIND

By **Kenneth Chisholm**

THE ULTIMATE BETRAYAL

By **Phoenix**

Frank Gresham

<u>BOOKS BY LDP'S CEO, CA$H</u>

TRUST NO MAN

TRUST NO MAN 2

TRUST NO MAN 3

BONDED BY BLOOD

SHORTY GOT A THUG

A DIRTY SOUTH LOVE

THUGS CRY

THUGS CRY 2

TRUST NO BITCH

TRUST NO BITCH 2

TRUST NO BITCH 3

TIL MY CASKET DROPS

Coming Soon

THUGS CRY 3

BONDED BY BLOOD 2

TRUST NO BITCH (KIAM & EYEZ' STORY)